THE
HAUNTING AT
2095

Rosella C. Rowe

GYPSY
PUBLICATIONS

Published in 2020, by Gypsy Publications
Troy, OH 45373, U.S.A.
www.GypsyPublications.com

Copyright © Rosella C. Rowe, 2020

First Edition

This story is based on the author's experiences in her childhood
house, located in Troy Ohio. The names of the characters have been
changed to protect their identities. The events recounted in this
book are retold to the best of the author's recollection and in light
of the research she conducted preparing to retell this story.

Rowe, Rosella C.
The Haunting at 2095 / by Rosella C. Rowe
ISBN 978-1-938768-95-8 (paperback)

For more information, please visit the author's
website at www.RosellaCRowe.com

DEDICATION

This book is dedicated to the woman who
lived in my house at 2095. I was meant to tell
your story so you could save others. Thank
you for guiding me through this journey.

— Rosella C. Rowe

FOREWORD

By Author Greg Enslen

I've been a fan of ghost stories for as long as I can remember. My first published book was a ghost story, filled with dread and foreboding. And while the novel is about two people reconnecting over time and distance, the underlying thread of a ghost tale deepens the mystery and casts a sinister tone over the whole story. People often ask me about the ghost in *The Ghost of Blackwood Lane*, and I think it's because people crave a good, well-written tale of ghosts, hauntings and apparitions. The main reason I included a ghost element in my book was because I've always been a fan of those types of stories.

And others love them as well—in fact, American Literature over the last two centuries has enjoyed a rich and vibrant history of tragedy and ghost stories. They harken back to a time of great mysteries, when the world around us was filled with unknown spaces and unknowable dangers. But, even in our "modern" age of miracles and technology, where we seemingly *KNOW EVERYTHING,* the power of a good ghost story still holds sway over modern audiences.

For most people, ghost stories are some of the first tales they hear growing up. Remember gathering around the campfire with your friends and family, sharing hot dogs, cocoa, and S'mores, just *WAITING* to turn in after a long day of camping? The ghost stories that accompany camping just seem like a natural thing, something to break up the monotony and pepper the camping experience with a scary tale or two. For me, growing up, the story that always got me was the one with the "escaped mental patient." For some reason, he always had a metal hook for a hand! I suppose that story probably got everyone, but it was *STILL* the fascination of the ghost story that always drew me in as a child—and, I confess, probably even as an adult. *Who doesn't like a good ghost story, right?*

But some ghost stories feel more real! Some of them you get part-way through and you put up your hand and say "Nope, that's it. I'm good." You don't want to hear the rest of the story…it's just too creepy! Or for some others, it hits a little *TOO* close to home!

The scariest ghost stories are the ones that feel real. In this case, Rosella C. Rowe's *The Haunting At 2095* sure feels real because it is real. The most frightening parts of the story are her retelling the events that took place in her childhood home, a seemingly normal house in a very normal town in suburban Ohio. The setting alone doesn't immediately lend itself to feelings of dread. The reader may be taken by surprise at the turn of events that occur over the course of the story.

Some of the scariest parts of Rosella's tale are the small moments. Home alone, hearing mysterious noises. Wondering if someone has entered the house. Whispered stories from neighbors of what happened in the house before they moved in. This is not a home that anyone would want to visit. You certainly wouldn't want to be the main character of this ghost story, home alone with your younger brother, wary of what might happen in a home that you are convinced is *OFF* in some way, even if you can't explain why. And then, when the events start, it's up to *YOU* to investigate them! Worse yet, no one believes you. How would you feel, trapped in a situation like that? I don't envy anyone who has had such an experience. Life can be scary enough without the creepy sound of jingling keys coming from somewhere in the house, over and over.

Rosella has done an amazing job bringing her story to life. Some of the scariest aspects of her story sent chills down my spine. I won't spoil it for you ahead of time but be warned—there are some seriously chilling aspects of her account of growing up in the house featured in this story. The idea that the story could be wrapped up in a positive fashion is amazing, considering what transpires!

One of my favorite aspects of the book was the way the narrative flips back and forth between the author's experiences and a larger backstory that serves to explain (and even foreshadow) what's happening in the main story. It's an excellent narrative structure that serves to ramp up the tension and keep the reader guessing, right up until the very end.

The first thing I thought after finishing the book was "wow, I can't believe all of these things happened to my friend," followed closely by the thought that no one should have to go through something like this, especially a child. I also reminded myself of another important piece of information: I needed to be nicer to Rosella in the future. Look at what she had to put up with growing up!

With *The Haunting At 2095*, Rosella C. Rowe has crafted a modern-day retelling of a classic ghost story, layering the narrative with shocking twists and taut action. She takes us on a harrowing journey into the history and horror of a seemingly normal suburban home, one that turns out to anything but normal.

Greg Enslen is the author of 28 books, including four books in the *Frank Harper Mysteries* series and three other novels. He has also written guides for popular TV shows like *Game of Thrones* and *Mr. Robot*.

THE HAUNTING AT 2095

This story is based on my experiences in the house, located in Troy Ohio, in which I grew up. I have changed some of the names to protect people's identities. The events recounted in this book are retold to the best of my recollection and in light of research I conducted preparing to retell this story.

PROLOGUE
Present Day

I stand outside the house numbered 2095 where I used to live looking at it in a cold, dead stare. It's an unseasonably warm November night as I linger here alone with the safety of my black SUV behind me.

What am I doing here? Who am I kidding? But I know. I always end up right here. Every Thanksgiving. Every Christmas Eve. So many random nights that have nothing to do with any warm-fuzzy sentiment. It's all the same: I stare at a house so familiar wishing it would stare back at me and smile. Or give me a kind of I-missed-you-too hug. But instead it just sits there cold and unfeeling, like I'd never been a part of it leaving me longing again.

And if I stand here long enough (*and I always do!*), this place also throws guilt and sadness at me. I feel so inexplicably sad. *Ok, that's understandable. But* w*hy does it insist I feel guilty? I have nothing to feel guilty about!*

The house mocks me and I can't turn away. I can't seem to move on from a place I simultaneously love and hate for fear *it* will abandon *me. Maybe I should let it and end this warped attachment.* I'm logical enough to know this dependence I have for an inanimate object is one-sided and not at all normal. But I also know this place, my house, the place of our shared existence, will never cease its presence in my mind. It's as if the house knows!

So, I'll continue to relive the same scenario: stand in front a house I no longer have a right to, and stare at it vacantly. *Observing? Guarding? Willing it to rewrite history?* I don't even know. It's just the same chapter with no ending in sight.

If I really think about it, this house that has become the heart of my fixation is relatively nondescript to the onlooker – a small ranch on a little hill. It's mostly light brown brick with an area of light brown siding in the front that sticks out from the rest of the home. Coordinating sage paint covers the wood trim around it and outlines the roll-out vertical windows. As I face the house, there's a large oak tree to the right and a sidewalk that winds from the front door all the way around back to a large, now overgrown, flower garden. Perennials had clearly been planted over the years so something bloomed year-round. You had no choice but to be drawn to the house – by its textures, colors, and quaintness.

As I look toward the long forgotten and browning flowers, so many questions roll through my mind. Yet, I don't know that I'd accept any answers offered. So I let my mind wonder where it will.

Look how big that tree has gotten! The scene before me unfolds with all its evidence of passing time. There are so many memories of that tree. I remember taking pictures for my dad on Father's Day under that tree. *The top branches weren't even as high as the roof of our house.* I remember my sister making us all dress up in our church best, then rounding us up. She had very specific ideas of where each of us should stand and how to smile. "Ok! Now everyone act natural!" *Was she kidding?* We were all standing under a tree! *We were happy beneath that tree.* I wore a little pink and white striped two-piece jumper. *I loved that outfit!* God only knows how old I was. What I do remember is feeling so very cute and happy, being all dressed up under that tree.

My eyes move from the tree to the huge rock that's the centerpiece of the flower garden. It seems to beam back at me in the moonlight. *Maybe something here does remember me!* My friend, Victoria, and I used to play on that rock – as if we could conquer anything just by climbing to the top of it, throwing our arms in the air, and stating a command. "I shall be ruler of this planet!" Victoria liked to proclaim. The rock seemed larger than life as a kid. Now looking at it, I see it's discolored and smooth with time, much of it underground. The truth is, when I really needed it, that rock didn't help me conquer a thing.

We played shopping mall, hide-and-seek, and king of the mountain. I can't even count the number of boys we pretend-married on that rock: walking down the garden path, *step-together-step-together-step-together,* with a fresh-picked bouquet of Mom's flowers and shriveled up dandelions. So many summers, so many joyful memories.

A smile widens across my face as the November breeze washes over me. I stick my chin up to feel the air's warmth and it all comes rushing back. And I long for those happy memories to stay. Unfortunately, just as rapidly as the pleasant memories flood my mind, the terrifying ones blindside me. THE FEAR ... HER!

The all too familiar streak of adrenaline replaces the calm throughout my body. *Not again.* Then I remember why I always end up here. It's not for the good memories. This reality is unwelcome. *Again.* The house feels like a homing device, luring me in for its own amusement. It draws me in to peacefully reminisce my happiest youthful memories, pouncing and twisting in my most terrifying childhood visions and insecurities.

Can she see me? Does she know I am here? Can she even remember me? I pause to think. *Did she even know who I was?* Another surge of adrenaline moves through me. This time starting at the bottom of my feet and flowing up through my body. A solid lump forms in my throat – a merging of dread, sadness, and regret – and it sticks there. Suddenly I can't breathe.

Gasping for air, I barely get out, "Oh, God," as I look toward the house. A tear passes down my cheek without thought to how much of my life it carries. It just falls. Others soon follow. It's dark and no one appears to be awake inside; at least, I don't see any movement.

I couldn't have gone through this for no reason; I can hardly think the words. *Could I?*

The wind picks up, seemingly angry, and causes the golden leaves to fall. They blow about, brushing past my face and I instinctively shut my eyes. My tears, now cold and heavy, silently make their way down my pale cheeks, each drop a weight lifted. A memory come and gone – again.

Flashes of her smiling face enter my mind. The way she looked at me while in my kitchen. *Our kitchen!* I can see her so clearly. *She was so clear as if she were right in front of me and I could reach out a hand and touch her.* Her crimson lipstick beamed from her face as she smiled at me. Her pale skin and blue eye shadow brought out the beauty in her light brown eyes. Those memorable facial features forever framed by her short, bobbed, brown hair. *Why was she there?* And after all these years, I can't help but wonder … *Is she still?*

MOVING DAY

I was ten years old when I, Becca Fletcher, moved into The House at address 2095 in a suburban neighborhood of Troy, Ohio. I hadn't moved far from where we had lived, maybe a mile. The house was beautiful, located on a nice street with wonderful neighbors who were always there for us. My father left us the year before, leaving my mother to buy her first house alone. I was one of the four children moving in. My sister and brother were teenagers, so each of them got their own room. I shared a room with my baby brother, Zander, just seven months old. I wasn't happy about moving and I *definitely* wasn't happy about sharing a room with a baby.

I remember that day like it was yesterday; July 3, 1990. It was a ridiculously hot summer day in southern Ohio. As I watched everyone move our personal belongings, I sat on my unmade bed petting our family dog, Gypsy, in the middle of our outdated dining room, which sadly became my new bedroom. The movers quickly trudged from the little rented truck parked in our new driveway to one of the rooms inside and put down another box.

Looking back, Mom was pretty scattered in those months (*maybe years?*) after the divorce, but she was at least organized; she had labeled all the boxes for easier moving.

There must have been fifteen people in and out of our house. The friends helping us move were so detached. They'd grab a box without thought to how much work had gone into packing it or how much sentiment was tucked inside, and they'd toss it through the front door. *Ok, so maybe they set some of the boxes down gently, but whatever.*

Boxes were still thrown all about. Closed boxes, open boxes, boxes tipped on their sides. Boxes upside down and right side up, and boxes where new tape covered old tape that was dry and crumbly and breaking off in pieces. So many boxes that didn't seem strong enough to even carry air. Boxes that came from recycling and boxes that should have stayed there. There were boxes with shredded paper protecting the few nice, glass items we had. *Ok, there's only one of those boxes.* There were tidy boxes neatly packed and then there were boxes that were packed like I felt – haphazardly thrown together with a mix of items from a mix of rooms, barely held together by cheap tape, then carelessly cast into a strange house. The junk drawer of boxes. The box no one looked in because it sat unopened in the basement for fifteen years until finally, one day, someone realized something was missing. Something they didn't even really need.

Is that really how I see myself?

I must have appeared pathetic, because everyone who passed by felt the need to "comfort" me with unwanted advice like, "This is for the best" and "Things are going to be just fine" and "Cheer up!" I didn't want their advice. I also didn't want to cheer up. I was angry! I just wanted to wallow in my self-pity and sadness and cry alone!

I remember how much I didn't want to be there and

how much I hated the whole world. Mostly I remember how much I hated my father, and how I blamed him for the entire ordeal.

However, later that same day, I met my future husband and his parents at our new neighborhood's Annual Fourth of July Block Party down the street. So, to say I hated that entire chapter of my life seems wrong. It was necessary. I had to move to meet the boy who would later comfort me through so many unexplainable events in that house. He would grow to become the man who would agree to comfort me for the rest of my life. It was meant to be.

But in July of 1990, I had no idea that my life would forever be changed by moving into 2095.

How Can I Tell Her?

November 1986

Tom pushed opened the door to leave work at the Goodrich plant in Troy, Ohio, as he had done every day for the past 3 years, but today the door felt heavy.

He took a few steps outside the brown, metal doors of the employee entrance and stopped in his tracks. Looking down at his feet, his head and body slumped over, Tom sighed. He dug his hand into the right-side pocket for his car keys and glanced up at the looming sky. It was a dark and windy day, with rain clearly on the horizon. The gray clouds hung low and heavy.

"Of course, it's going to rain," Tom said aloud to no one.

He didn't want to go home. He didn't want to tell her the worst good news of their lives. *God, why did this have to happen?* The dread started as soon as he was told, and it never went away. *When I tell her, it'll completely destroy a world she loves.*

THE WALTER HOUSE

"Whooooo ... Spooky," I say as my friend, Stacey, leaps out at me in our dark hallway near the bathroom. She's trying hard to scare me as we tell ghost stories. I'm actually more freaked out by the dark hallway than her, but I let her believe I'm scared anyway to make her happy.

"You were scared!" insists Stacey.

But I know I'm not. She's too predictable. Not to mention, I could hear her breathing from around the corner. *God, she's a loud breather!*

As I walk back down the dark, looming hallway into our family room, Stacey follows. We plop down on the couch beside Heather, the babysitter. Heather is actually only three years older than me, but Mom still thinks I'm too young at 11 years old, to be home without an adult and be responsible for my little brother, Zander. Heather's pretty cool so I guess it's ok. She mostly does homework and makes sure we're still alive when Mom gets home from work.

We laugh, being typical silly girls. Our ghost stories are fresh in our minds as Halloween had just passed. Heather looks up at us. "I can't believe you two are joking around about ghosts and trying to scare each other in this house! You've got to be crazy!"

Stacey and I look at each other, confused. "What?" I ask.

"Yeah, what are you talking about?" Stacey asks, following my lead.

Heather looks up from her books, pushes her glasses up on her nose, and suddenly looks serious.

With a straight face, she attempts to explain, "Everyone knows about this house. You know, Mrs. Walter and the garage. The last thing you want to do is tick her off!"

Stacey and I are just as confused after Heather's explanation as we were before.

"Who is this Mrs. Walter, and how does everyone know about her?"

"Um, what are you talking about?"

"You mean you seriously don't know?" Heather asks with a serious tone.

"No, I really have no idea what you're talking about," I say.

Then it dawns on me; she's just trying to scare us. Heather can be a drama queen. She's even going to major in theater at college and talks about it every chance she gets. She's constantly reading classic novels and fake acting them out. This is probably her just trying to pull our legs for a bit of fun.

So, I call her on it. "Wait a minute. Are you just trying to scare us?" My voice is cocky enough to let her know I'm on to her, but just in case, I also turn to Stacey with a "Yeah, sure. This is true" look on my face.

However, as I turn back to face Heather, a tingle of fear causes the hair on my arms to stand on end. She's looking me dead in the eyes, with an unmistakable seriousness, as she sits with her feet folded under her and her hands crossed over her chest just staring at me. Her odd gaze goes through me as I suddenly notice her dark features looking more prominent than ever.

For once, Stacey and I are speechless. We don't move a muscle, as we wait for her to speak.

"Why would I make this up, Becca?" she says, in a low deep voice. "What would I possibly have to gain?"

Just then, a tiny tingle of fear turns into a lump in my throat as I recognize truth in Heather's voice. Moving slowly, Heather sets aside her textbooks and pencil before looking back up at us. What she saw on our faces must have told her we were prepared to listen. She continued.

"Mrs. Walter was the woman who lived in your house before you and your family. I remember she had kids. I can't remember how many or their ages, but they were little. They had the two bedrooms behind this wall." Heather twists slightly on the couch to tap the wall behind her. She drops her hand to her lap and continues.

"She was married, and as I recall, she seemed ok as a neighbor. But she didn't seem very happy right before they moved. I only know what I've heard. But anyway, she lived here before you guys, and killed herself right here in this house."

"What!" I screech out uncontrollably, as I jump up from my seat on our blue velvet couch.

"Yeah. Actually, right behind you," Heather tells us, as she looks over my shoulder and points behind me.

Stacey and I slowly turn as if we're about to see an actual ghost or something even more horrifying right behind us. We can't *NOT* look! We follow Heather's pointed finger with our eyes toward our kitchen.

"The kitchen?" I ask, in a shaking voice.

"No, the garage!"

"Garage?" says Stacey, in a shaky voice.

"Yep!" Heather replies with the confidence of

a teenager who knows everything. And she's all too pleased to continue sharing her knowledge on the unfortunate subject.

"That's why this house took forever to sell! Rightly," she added, with even more confidence. "No one wants to live in a house where a lady killed herself! But then your mom bought it, and now you guys are the first to live here since 'the incident.'"

Stacey and I look at each other. Our eyes lock and we're both too afraid to move or make a sound. We just sit in my small family room horrified and confused.

Heather breaks the silence, "Don't worry. I'm sure it's fine!"

Sure! I think sarcastically. *I just found out that some strange woman killed herself in my house! Yeah, everything's just great! How can she sit there and say that everything is just fine after telling us that?*

"Becca?" Stacey's voice breaks through my thoughts. "I have an idea of what we can do. It'll be fun!" Stacey suddenly grabs my wrist, ignoring Heather and our surroundings, and pulls me up from the couch.

Thank goodness. I may have sat there forever in stunned silence.

As Stacey leads me out of the family room and through the house's little foyer to the living room, we see Heather pick her textbooks up again to study. Like she hadn't just dropped a bomb in our laps.

I watch in a trance-like state as Stacey pats around the wall in the dark room, to find the new light switch my grandfather just installed. The floor light comes on and the yellow hue on the cream-colored carpet casts just enough light to see the L-shaped white silk couch that lines the wall like a shadow. Just seeing the light is calming.

"Thanks for getting us out of that room, Stacey."

"I'm sure it isn't true, Becca." Stacey whispers so Heather doesn't hear us. She tries to reassure me as she puts her hand on my shoulder for comfort. "I'm sure she's just trying to freak us out." Stacey reassures me to get me to snap me out of my fear. "You know, I'm sure Heather has nothing better to do. She's stuck here babysitting and probably bored with homework, so we're her entertainment. She's just messing with us because she's bored!"

I consider this. Maybe Heather is just joking and pulling our legs. I'll bet she is having a good laugh right now at our expense. Typical teenager!

But it doesn't matter how many different ways I try to talk myself into it. My gut is calling my bluff.

"Maybe you're right. But she did look pretty serious."

"Yeah, I know. You think there's a chance it could really be true?"

BRINGING HOME THE BAD NEWS

Lifting his head back up and rolling his shoulders a little, Tom came back to reality and started to look around the large parking lot for his car. He looked back and forth a few times, before finally eyeing his black BMW far out on the left side of the lot.

I won't miss this huge parking lot! Tom thought, as he strolled toward his car.

As he walked, a cold raindrop plopped on his head right in the middle of his scalp. He looked up to the heavens and prayed that God would help his wife and family tonight and help them prepare for the huge changes to come.

Poor Kyle, sighed Tom, as his head sank down, and the weight of the world landed squarely on his shoulders. *How will he handle this?* Tom picked up his head again and realized he was already in front of his car. He was so shaken by his thoughts and worries, that he hadn't even noticed he'd walked clear across the lot.

Will life ever be normal again, or will this ruin my family forever? He just stood there, staring into the window of his car wondering and questioning as rain soaked him. *What am I going to do? Wait, I can't think that. I have to go! It's my only option if I want to stay with the company.*

Tom took his car keys out of the pocket of his black trench coat and inserted one into the keyhole in the driver's side door. Twisting it until the door clicked, Tom swung open the black door of his car and slumped down. He gripped the steering wheel like it was his lifeline.

Everything was running smoothly at home and things with Kyle had been going so well for months. *Now here I come to drop this bomb.*

Tom lifted his hands, covering his face in sorrow. *Why do we have to uproot our lives now?* A promotion was fantastic, but his gut already knew this wasn't going to be good for his family.

Tom sat with his hands covering his face for several minutes, feeling even worse about the task ahead. *Sitting here won't make it go away.* He surely couldn't face her like this. He needed to calm down and pull himself together before starting home. There simply wasn't a good way to prepare for this, or for the events that will likely follow.

This evening's news wasn't just going to temporarily change their lives. It would devastate his family permanently.

Would they ever be able to forgive him?

THE HALLWAY

Thump, thump. Thump, thump …

Who is that? "Ughhhh … I don't want to get up and go look." I complain out loud.

It's nine o'clock at night and I'm in bed reading my assigned novel of the month for English class when I hear the sounds coming from the hall. *It's probably my sister.* I think she said she was going to her friend's. That was an hour or so ago, so she must have left already. It can't be my older brother, because he moved out a month ago, which is how I got the big bedroom at the end of the hall. After all I am 13 now; however, my mother says I act like I'm 30! She thinks she is so funny.

It's now 1993 on a cold winter night. It's freezing in the house, as always. "God, I hate this house. It's always so cold," I say aloud, as I find my slippers and wrap up in my long fleece robe hanging on my bedpost. *This better be worth it.*

Dressed in my robe and shuffling my slippered feet toward the door, I hear the sound again.

Thump, thump. Thump, thump …

Man, if she keeps up that noise or whatever she's doing, she's going to wake up Zander! I've already put him to bed once, and I'm not doing it again! If she wakes him up, she can put him back to sleep herself!

As I pull open the door, a wave of cold air hits me in

the face, all my hair stands up on end and a shiver goes up my spine. No lights are on in the house. The hall is pitch black. *Good grief we need a nightlight out here!*

"What?!" I yell out loud, as I yank open the door the rest of the way and step out into the hall.

No one.

The bathroom is to the left of my bedroom and so is the closest light I can turn on. I quickly reach inside the door feeling for the switch and flip it on, casting just enough light down the hall.

Maybe Zander got up? But as I look around and listen, I don't see or hear anyone. No shadows; no sounds.

Obviously, no one is up. But just in case, I call with a shaky voice, "Hello? Is anyone there?" I wait for an answer but don't hear a response. I muster up the strength to walk into my brother's bedroom.

"Zander?" I whisper as I walk into his room. I don't want to wake him if he is sleeping through the light and noise.

"Zander?" I repeat, as I get closer to his blue bunk bed. When I see him in his bed, I nearly faint! There he is, warm and snuggled up in his favorite blanket, fast asleep. He doesn't even flinch when I say his name, or notice the light pouring into his room.

That's when it hits me – I'm alone in the house, responsible for my little brother's safety on a Friday night, and someone else, an uninvited some else, must be in our house.

I walk back out into the hall, panic-stricken. *Should I call my mother? I don't even remember where she said she was going! Okay, Plan B.* Calling is obviously out since I have no idea where to call. I take in a big breath to calm myself and listen again for someone in the house. *Maybe whoever it is will make another noise.*

Nothing.

That's good!

No, wait, that could be bad! They could be hiding in the dark! Oh my God, I don't even know what to think. I continue tiptoeing down the hall. I exhale slowly and listen even harder – if that was even possible!

Nothing.

Other than my own pounding heartbeat.

Now I panic. Maybe I can't hear them because they're on the other side of the house by now, hiding quietly in a corner somewhere just waiting to attack in the darkness!

Oh God! Mom's room! It's on the other side of the house, I think as I creep toward her room.

"Hello?" I call, my voice giving away my fears.

And again, I hear nothing.

Alright. Be brave and go see!

Shaking in fear, as I walk around looking near our couches and crouch down to the floor to peek under the end tables. I pass through the family room. However, I still don't see anyone or hear any movement.

Finally, I reach my mom's room and really, really don't want to go in! *If I were a burglar, this is where I'd hide – close to the front door for a quick get-away.* I take another big breath, and step into her bedroom.

I walk in slowly and go directly for her light switch and flip it on. The overhead light immediately fills the room. I'm ready for something, someone to jump out from behind mom's bed. But … nothing. As I wait, I scan the room. When my eyes get to her bathroom, I remember her walk-in closet. *Another perfect hiding place. Ugh!* My panic floods back!

My throat feels like it's swelling up so much that I can't breathe. *No more calming breaths for me.* I put on my brave face and walk into my mother's bathroom. Now isn't the best time to realize I have no way of defending myself, yet here I am, defenseless.

Where is anyone in this dumb family when you need them?

My feet sink into the plush white carpet while I look around. And yet again, I don't see anyone, or hear a single sound.

Nothing. The silence is deafening!

I take one step, then another, and another, inching toward the closet where the mass of clothes could easily conceal someone. *Keep calm and breathe.*

If my mind would pull it together and stay quiet long enough, maybe I could think rationally! *It certainly isn't giving me any helpful advice!* I am barely a teenager and solely responsible for a little boy. *If there is someone in that closet, what on earth will I do to protect us?*

My courage flares at that thought. *I have to defend Zander! He's my responsibility!* I put my hand on the doorknob. *Fight or flight sure is real!* Then I twist.

I blow out a large breath I didn't realize I'd been holding; it feels like my lungs may explode. I want to cry and run in the other direction. Or perhaps, kick, hit, or throw something. But I don't have time for that now. I must look inside this closet.

The question of the mysterious sounds and possible stranger will be left unanswered and will scare me all night long. I'll never get any sleep, until I get this over with! *Who am I kidding, I won't sleep now either way.*

In a flash, I push open the door and quickly grab the dangling string that is the light switch, pulling hard as I turn on the walk-in closet light.

Nothing.

Are you kidding me?

I can't tell if I'm disappointed that a stranger didn't

immediately jump out at me, or if I'm petrified, realizing now I have to search behind all those clothes and boxes. *I don't think I can take anymore!*

Suddenly, I shriek and the sound of the garage opening snaps me back to my senses. I peel myself off the ceiling (*okay, I didn't jump THAT high*) then peek out through the bathroom into my mother's bedroom. I see her car headlights as they blissfully light up the whole room. Unfortunately, that also means I don't have long to search before she gets inside the house.

I turn back to her closet. Nothing seems out of place. Aggressively, I attack the clothes on the racks, feeling all around and searching behind them all. I drop to the floor and look under the racks around her shoes but find no sign of anyone having been here. Except for the hallway noise, I have nothing!

"What the ... UGH!" I yell, more confused than ever. *What the hell is happening? Someone HAD to make that noise and I know it wasn't Zander or me! Who else is in this house??*

Hearing a familiar noise, I jump up and grab the light switch string, giving it a quick tug. Turning off the light, I sneak out of the large closet and back into my mother's room.

"Becca, you scared me!" cried my mother breathing hard in surprise, as I rounded the corner into her bedroom. "What are you doing up, with all the lights on?"

"I honestly don't know!" I answered, as I shrugged my shoulders.

HOME

About 6 p.m. Tom pulled up the driveway's small hill and put his car in park. But he didn't turn it off right away. He sat there looking at his house, thoughts whirling through his head, dreading going inside. He knew his wife, Julia, must have heard his car pull in. She was probably placing food on the table for dinner, as he sat there stalling. Dusk was coming fast.

Tom turned the car key to the left and heard the BMW's engine turn off. Never removing his hold on the key, Tom sat motionless as he took in their home. Any other person perhaps wouldn't appreciate their little home. But he and his family did. People would probably just stroll down the street, or pass by in their vehicles without a second glance. What may have appeared plain to them was special to him and his family.

So many little touches that he didn't necessarily value day-to-day now made him emotional. Tom glanced over the yard he worked so hard on, and the garden with the big rock that the kids loved to play on. And the flowers Julia gathered and planted with so much thought and love last spring.

Little Thomas loved to dig in the mud with his toy truck, while Julia planted flowers or weeded the large garden. She usually planted tulips and pansies, her favorites. He remembered how happy she seemed digging into the earth with her bare hands, a few gardening tools by her side. She designed the layout of the plants and flowers around the rock, so the color blossomed evenly throughout the bed. But the best trick was that the kids could play on the rock, without trampling and killing the flowers. *How did she have the foresight to know they'd want to play there?* It was love. *She loved this place.*

Julia waved to neighbors across the street or next door every day and to anyone strolling through the neighborhood as they walked by the house. *She was always happy and friendly.* She got to know everyone! She'd give a friendly hello and maybe chat for a few moments, then get on with her to-do list, but she always took time for others. If a neighbor was sick, she was the first person at his or her door with homemade chicken noodle soup and chamomile tea.

Sitting there, he realized he hadn't even walked out to the garden this year. He always thought they would have time for those types of things when they retired and the kids were grown and gone. Now it felt like he had wasted valuable time.

The house was a lovely brick ranch, with an alcove by the front door that stuck out, and where the sidewalk to the garden started. The tan wood paneling near the front entrance was bordered by long vertical windows that rolled outward, trimmed with light green paint.

A small oak tree on the right side of the yard was barely a decade old, but it was their favorite shady spot to sit for pictures. Each annual Easter photo evidenced the tree's and their kids' growth. Also evident was the bounty of treats found during the egg hunt. The kids, with wide, bright smiles, always had their loot at their feet or overflowing from their arms. You could also see a repeat of Kyle's past Easter outfits each year, because Thomas would wear Kyle's hand-me-downs. Julia and Tom always chuckled about that after each photo was taken, while gathering the kids and their goodies off the grass and shooing everyone back inside the house.

And the neighbors – the Davises, Hutchinses, and the Smiths – were always there when you needed them. Sometimes, they even showed up when you didn't know you needed them, with food, a drink, or just a, "Hey-how-you-doin?" The value of those times became clearer with every passing year. *I could sure go for some of Mrs. Hutchins's lemon cookies.*

Mr. Davis, on the other hand, may have looked like a simple middle-aged man with a little gray in his dark jet-black hair, but he wasn't. Not when it came to holidays. He truly made Halloween and the Fourth of July special for all of the neighborhood's kids.

At Halloween, he would make a haunted house out of large trash bags and tarps in his front yard, and play scary screaming Halloween tapes out his windows. Sometimes he would dress up like a scarecrow covered in fake blood and jump out at the trick-or-treaters as they rounded a corner of his makeshift haunted house. Somehow, he managed to scare and humor everyone.

On the Fourth, Mr. Davis coordinated a neighborhood lawn mower race, and hand-made an archway by welding a bent water pipe and drilling holes in it. He hooked up his garden hose to the pipe and water would come down through the archway, falling onto kids and their big wheels as they rode or walked through. Everyone referred to it as the "Kiddie Carwash," and he genuinely enjoyed setting it up bright and early on mower race day. Mr. Davis was the nicest neighbor Tom ever had, with Tom wishing Mr. Davis had been a mentor when Tom was a child, just so he could hang out in Mr. Davis's garage with him. He was always tinkering in that garage. On what, who knows? But Mr. Davis always was calm, content, and kind. *And we could all use a little more of that in the world.*

It was time. God only knew how long he'd been daydreaming, reminiscing … and dreading what was to come. Tom only knew he had to go inside and face his family. He'd avoided it for far too long and knew his wife would be upset with his dilly-dallying.

So, he sighed as he stepped out of the car.

He had big news that was GREAT, except for the moving part. *So, not completely good news.* After today, she'd be okay. Julia was a reasonable person. She'd be upset, sure; this was not expected, not part of their life plan and he knew she didn't want to move again so soon. Who wouldn't be upset? But then she'd rationalize it and we could move on to have a good, happy life! *Yep, everything will be fine,* he told himself.

Talking himself into believing all would be well, Tom walked through his garage to the door leading into the house.

Turning the doorknob, he stepped into the kitchen and called out to his family, "Hi, everyone! I'm home!"

As Tom shut the door behind him, he dumped his stuff on the floor, as usual, behind an antique table near the window. *So far so good. Just breathe.*

Tom looked up and spotted his curly-haired brunette wife standing in front of the kitchen counter making dinner. She was beautiful as always, wearing a blue apron that brought out her pale blue eyes and familiar red lipstick. However, tonight she seemed very displeased. She had a cream-colored spatula in her hand as she slowly began to move something brown and sizzling around in a saucepan.

"Where have you been, Tom?" she said with a quick frustrated glance, before turning back to her task at hand.

"Gosh, I'm sorry. I'll make it up to you later."

"Well, whether you do or not, I think dinner is ruined. I hope you like burnt Sloppy Joes and fries." Julia's small crimson painted mouth was frowning, as she hastily shuffled food onto plates. Her beautiful eyes accented with light blue shadow and brown eyeliner were adorable, even when scrunched up in anger, as she served blackened fries from a pan with one hand and grabbed napkins with the other.

"Sure, symbolizes my day," Tom muttered under his breath. But he might as well have said it in a regular voice because his wife's keen ear heard him.

"What?" she barked back, even though she knew.

"Nothing. I'm sorry. It's just been a day, that's all. Don't worry about it."

His wife grabbed condiments for the table and walked to the dining room.

"Kids! Dinner!" she shouted over her shoulder.

As Tom turned, he saw one medium and one tall streak run past him through the kitchen and into the dining room. They were all too happy to sit down to a prepared meal, doing none of the work. *Too bad they never tell their mother that.*

AGAIN

"Your turn," I say as my friend, Emily, and I play *Truth or Dare* while lying on my bed. A nightlight in the far corner of my bedroom is the only glow breaking up the darkness. We've been laughing and giggling about typical teenage girl nonsense for hours, no longer frightened by the darkness of our surroundings.

My bedroom is the furthest from the family room, so we hope our chatter isn't keeping everyone else awake. But it's also a freezing February night and this end of the house is by far the coldest. Emily and I put on our flannel pajamas to stay warm and eventually struggle to stay awake, closing our eyes in between jokes, and sinking further into my bed.

"Okay, so who would you rather marry: Jonathon Brandis from the TV Show, *SeaQuest* or Scott McCarthy from school?

Now I'm wide awake.

"Well, of course, Jonathon Brandis!" I snap back and we both squeal in laughter.

"Okay, Jason Jacobs or Mark Snider from school?"

"Mark Snider!" we both say at the same time as we high five each other.

"Adam Starkey or Christopher McMurray?"

"Ewwww for both! We clearly need cuter boys in our class."

After a few more minutes of giggling and asking

random *Truth or Dare* questions, we're interrupted by a huge thud.

We grab hold of each other and sit straight up in my bed.

"What was that?" Emily asks.

"I don't know," I tell her. "It sounded like it was near the door. Maybe it's my sister in the bathroom. She probably knocked something over."

"I think it came from in here, Becca. It sounded too loud to be in the bathroom."

"Yeah … I don't know. Something might have fallen off my dresser I guess." My head spins trying to come up with something logical that could have made that sound; but I come up with nothing and am tired of trying to. "I don't know. But I'm sleepy, so let's just call it a night."

"Want to look?" asks Emily.

"No! Do you?"

"Are you kidding?" she says. "It's not MY house!"

"Well, I'm sure it was nothing," I say, acting as if it really was nothing and trying to forget about the noise. "Who would you rather have as a lab partner in science class: Jonathan Brandis or Scott?"

"Both!" We laugh and soon forget all about the loud sound.

****

Thump, Thump, Thump

I don't know how long we've been asleep, but I wake up to another noise. Sitting up with a jolt, I try to figure out, again, what could have made such a sound.

Thump, thump

I hear it a second time, and now I'm afraid. I can

feel the adrenaline rush through my body, first in my stomach then shooting up through my chest, and then filling my head. *Oh, no! Not again!*

As I wait in the darkness for another sound, I can hardly breathe. I can't move. And suddenly, the walls feel like they are closing in on me. As I struggle for breath, I snuggle up closer to Emily. *It hasn't woken her yet.*

A few minutes go by and I don't hear anything else. Soon I start to wonder if I'd heard anything at all and slowly feel myself drifting back to sleep when …

Crack!

Another loud noise, but this one is different. This noise came from my door itself, exploding like someone took a baseball bat to my door from the other side.

Emily and I both jump out of our skin.

"Oh, my God!" she cries. "What was that?"

"I don't know!" I reply. "There have been a few noises, but this one's different. It seems closer and even angrier, if that's a possibility. Plus, it's definitely louder."

We're too terrified to even scream for help. We just hold on to each other like a lifeline and wait to hear if it happens again.

Then suddenly, it dawns on me. "Oh my gosh! I am so stupid!" I say as I throw my arms up in the air and my legs over the side of the bed. I grab my robe and stomp toward the door.

"Becca!" cries out Emily. "Are you crazy! What are you doing?" I can hear the panic in her voice as she tries to grab me and pull me back. "You could get hurt!"

"No, it's okay!" I say to her with a newfound confidence. "I'll bet it's my sister, Maggie, playing a joke on me since you're here tonight." Then I walk blindly through the dark room toward my bedroom door. "It would totally be like her to wait until I have a friend sleeping over to make a fool of me and scare us. I'm sure she thinks it's so funny. Maggie has a real 'got you' ego. Big sisters are like that. She's probably laughing like crazy right now. I'm sure I'll hear it for days: 'I can't believe how scared you two were! I really got you two good!' In fact, I'll bet that Maggie is right outside my door!"

"Oh … she did say, 'Sweet dreams you two' before she left for work."

I quickly flip the switch and the light pops on in my room as Emily hops out of bed. We meet at my doorway.

We look around the room to make sure nothing is out of place, then turn to face the dark wooden door.

"Alright, she has to be on the other side waiting to bang on it and scare us again," I whisper to Emily, certain of my sister's warped sense of humor.

"Right."

We stare at the door for another minute and then look back at each other, realizing that one of us has to open it.

"Alright, open the door," I say as I look at my friend.

"What?" Emily cries out in surprise, "It's your sister. YOU open it!"

Darnit, she has a point. "Okay …" I say and then I take a deep breath.

Certain that Maggie's pulling a prank on us, I slowly twist the doorknob, so she won't hear us coming for her.

Emily is holding her breath, while she waits for me to finish turning the knob. When it won't turn any more,

I nod to her. Frightened, Emily holds onto my back like a baby koala holds onto its mother and we brace ourselves for whatever is on the other side. *I'm going to kill Maggie for this!* I fling open my bedroom door ready for my sister's reaction.

"What the …" Emily trails off as she cocks her head to the right in confusion and then looks back at me.

Nothing! Both of us are shocked at what we are looking at…total darkness. No one was there. The hallway is dark and silent.

DINNER

Julia placed all the plates of food for her family's dinner in their appropriate spots and sat down with a long sigh. She was hardly aware she had even let a sigh escape.

"Geez, Mom," came her daughter's voice, as Sara plopped her 7-year-old body down at the family's table. She immediately grabbed for the large bottle of ketchup without asking her mother to pass it and started squeezing ketchup onto her plate.

The table might have been neatly set, but no one appreciated the effort. No one waited for anyone else to sit down. They all muttered to themselves and dug into the food without saying: 'Looks good, Mom!' Or even a, 'Thanks, Mom!' It was like she was invisible sometimes.

Julia looked at Sara after her harsh remark. "What did you say?" she asked her daughter, hoping she heard her wrong, just this once.

"I'd hardly call this a feast, so I don't know why you're sighing," Sara said. She raised her brown eyes to the ceiling in distaste, smirking in her mother's direction, as she began eating the food prepared by the target of her hostility. The words and actions were so ugly coming from a child; her light blonde hair pulled back by a baby blue headband, that she just *had* to have. The innocent-looking child didn't resemble the personality inside.

Julia was hardly shocked by Sara's comment. And not shocked at all by her actions. She learned it from her older brother; Tom and Julia obviously hadn't done a good job at stopping it. She always regretted that. *We teach people how to treat us.* Julia knew this. Unfortunately, she didn't feel equipped to change it. Not physically, not emotionally. It was especially hard when Tom wasn't ever there to help or back her up. So, Julia just went on ignoring the comments. It wasn't worth the effort (*the fight*), to correct them when she didn't have support.

Julia took the ketchup bottle when Sara was done and squeezed some out onto 4-year-old Thomas's plate. "Here you go, honey. For dipping," she told him, as she handed her son a napkin. He was still figuring out which condiments he liked, but one thing was certain – he loved dipping. He often experimented with multiple colors and flavors – sometimes mixing, sometimes not. Sometimes he just wanted some on his plate, but never intended to eat it. Sometimes he wanted ketchup and mustard and ranch but didn't want them to touch. Then there were some nights he didn't even want to see the bottles on the table. It was definitely a hit or miss thing. Tonight, Thomas ignored her and played with a toy instead of eating. This would mean extra work for Julia, as she would have to prompt him every few minutes to get him to eat his food. She wasn't looking forward to the battle.

Thomas was her sweet baby. He loved his toy cars, and, as long as he ate a bite of food now and then when Julia reminded him, she was fine with the toy at the table.

However, he was still potty-training, which had

been a battle, but she finally found something to motivate him – a new car. Julia was so proud of his progress. Thomas was actually paying attention to the chart and recognized when he had enough stars for a new HotWheel. He was so adorable, and boy did he know it. That dark brown hair was definitely from his daddy's side of the family; when he smiled, Thomas got anything he wanted from his mommy.

Really, it wasn't just that he had her wrapped around his finger, Thomas actually listened to her. If she asked him to pick up toys, or help clear the dishes after dinner, he did it. No whining. No "forgetting." No need to be asked five times to help. He just did what she asked. It was so nice!

Thomas was also the one who didn't want to see her cry. He was such a sweet and loving child. Julia always tried to hold it together, but sometimes the day was just too emotionally draining, and she found herself hiding for a good cry, alone. If Thomas found her, he'd offer to bring her a car, or sit with her and read one of the board books he'd memorized. It was very refreshing to see at least ONE of their children was empathetic! But it saddened Julia that such a young child felt the need to comfort his mom. It was not supposed to be that way.

Julia finally took the bottle and gave herself a little ketchup for her fries, then put her fallen sloppy Joe sandwich back together. As she picked it up to take a bite, she noticed Tom staring off into space. He was often tired when he got home from work, but he usually maintained some sort of conversation during dinner. This wasn't like him. He was slouched over the table with a blank look on his face, and he looked glum. Then Julia noticed he still hadn't touched his food, or even asked for the ketchup to be passed.

What is going on?

Julia and Tom never had what you could call a close or intimate relationship like other couples. Tom was career driven, Type-A. He had a great work ethic and loved his job. He liked his coworkers and boss, and didn't seem to mind traveling out of town when needed. Tom was always looking for the next promotion or the next big deal. *Why so vacant tonight?*

Tom was generally way more ambitious than Julia could ever be. He got up at every day at 5 a.m. to jog and was already showered and gone before Julia's alarm even went off or the kids got up for school. Sometimes it felt like two strangers living together, rather than a marriage.

Julia was often alone. She relied on her children to fill the void, but that usually didn't work. They didn't seem to care about her unless they needed a meal cooked or a snack made on demand after school. Except Thomas. No one seemed to notice her much. Was that her fault, or had that just happened? She wasn't sure, but it was getting worse.

Julia used to be close to her parents, but after the kids came along life got busy. They grew farther apart. With the kids' after school events and activities, her housework and her night nursing job, she didn't speak to them as often as she would have liked.

"Mom!?"

Julia snapped back to reality at the sound of their son, Kyle's, voice. She'd been deep in thought for several minutes. Looking at Tom she saw no difference. He still hadn't looked up. He just sat there, unmoving.

Kyle was sitting next to his father in a long-sleeved black t-shirt and black jeans. His jet-black hair only added to his dark demeanor. And he was irritated.

"Mom!" he demanded, "Where are the baked beans I asked for?" His pale face looked angrier with each word.

"Oh," started his mother looking at him, suddenly very tired, "I was in such a hurry after your father got home, that I forgot to make them. I'm so sorry, honey; I'll remember next time."

"Whatever." Kyle pushed his chair from their dining table and stood up. Taking his plate, he headed toward the kitchen sink and dumped his plate of food. "I am out of here," he said with hostility as he made his way to his room.

"Sorry again, honey!" Julia shouted after him.

Looking back at her husband for some support, some relief in handling Kyle, she noticed he was still zoned out, staring into space. Something was surely going on. *Maybe something happened at work.* She had never seen him like this before. *Maybe he was fired!* She had to ask.

"Tom, what's on your mind, dear?"

Her voice jolted Tom out of his trance. He shook his head, as if trying to wake from a daze, then looked at his wife across the table.

THE NEXT DAY

Emily and I woke up the next morning to a bright and sunny winter day, as if last night's trauma never happened.

Emily's mother is picking her up this afternoon, so we have plenty of time to hang out. However, I'm sure she'd rather be anywhere but at my house right now.

As we consider getting out of my warm, comfortable bed, we look at each other in silent debate. The frightening memory of last night is way too fresh. I can't help but wonder what really happened. *Was it just Maggie playing a trick on us?*

"Morning!" my mother's voice intrudes my thoughts, as she opens the bedroom door and sticks her head in. "Are you girls ever getting out of bed? I made waffles, so come and get 'em!" She pulls the door closed behind her.

Emily and I still haven't spoken. We lie in my bed frozen by our own fears and questions about last night; we really don't want to move from our safety zone.

"Now that we've had a chance to sleep on it, do you think it was your sister making the noise last night?" I can still see the fear and confusion in her eyes.

"I don't know," I reply honestly, still confused myself. "I don't know what happened, but I'm going to figure it out." Now that it's daylight we can dig a little deeper into what happened and see if Maggie was the person behind it.

We put on our robes, and I reach under my bed to pull out my slippers. Emily is already at my door waiting so we can walk down the hall for breakfast. At first, I think she's waiting for me out of courtesy. But then I see the slightest tremor in her hands and realize she's waiting for *me* to open the door.

I reach for the doorknob. "Alright, my mother's out there, so it's going to be fine," I say trying to reassure her (*and myself*). Flashbacks from last night are surprisingly hard to shake. A few hours ago, my hand was on the same doorknob dreading to see who or what was on the other side.

Taking one quick look back at Emily, I grab the knob with all the courage I can muster. It doesn't matter that sweat is pouring from my hand, or that the only encouragement I see is my friend's terrified face. But I do it – I throw open my bedroom door ... with my eyes closed. *Super brave, Becca. Like opening a door is hard. Good grief!*

"Alright, it's open!" I proclaim, and we both open our eyes.

This time the hallway is still empty, but at least it's not dark. No one is there. As daylight trickles down the long hall, we can see we're alone and we both let out a sigh of relief.

"Okay," I say, and we both stand straight up to compose ourselves, "Let's go." Slowly, we venture down the hall, taking baby steps as if we're tip-toeing somewhere forbidden. Periodically, I look back to see if my friend is still there, *mostly to make sure that I'm not alone.*

"It's alright," I tell her as I reach back for her hand. *Holding hands feels way safer.* We continue to walk a little hunched over, and Emily is almost on my back, as we try to breathe quietly knowing we're both probably breathing heavier than ever. As we reach the end of the hallway, another thought enters my mind. Someone might still jump out at us, at the end of the hall!

Paranoid! That's what we are now, paranoid! Its daylight and we haven't heard a strange noise in hours, but we jump at every sound.

"Hi guys!" says my mother, as she rounds the corner in a chipper voice.

"Ahhhhh!" Emily and I scream as we tumble to the ground tangled up with one another, not willing to let go. Then we realize my mom is talking to us and we look up.

"What in the world are you girls doing?" asks my mother, as she watches us scramble on the carpeted hall floor trying to separate and stand. "Are you two playing a game or something?"

We look at my mother who thinks we're nuts at this point. She is five feet, three inches tall, wearing jeans with a pumpkin orange sweater that has little pockets at the bottom sides. Her sweater really brings out her red hair and brown freckles lighting up her tanned skin after the long summer.

"Honey, what you are doing?" questions my mother again, her voice is starting to sound a little concerned.

Realizing I'm expected to say something, I look at Emily as we awkwardly lift ourselves off the floor, stand next to my mother and smile with slight embarrassment.

"Just thought we heard something. That's all." Emily and I stand up even straighter, as we try to smile weakly. *I'm sure this looks perfectly (ab)normal.*

My mother cracks a smile. "You silly, girls!" Then

she turns and walks away heading into the kitchen, thankfully gone from sight.

"What do we do now?" I hear Emily say. She has reattached herself to my arm and I feel her nails digging into my skin. My friends' anxiety stirs my anger.

How dare someone try to scare us like this! She'll never want to come back! She can't NOT come back again. She's my BEST FRIEND! I think of how scared Emily is and how hard it will be to convince her to ever spend the night again! No way is she going to want to come back to this spooky house!

"Becca, are you alright?" Emily's voice breaks through my thoughts.

"Yes," I say. But I'm not. Inside I feel like stomping around, screaming, and punching something.

I will not be afraid of my sister and her pranks anymore. She may have won last night but never again!

Emily watches me intently, as I consider our options. We're both engrossed deep in thought, when my sister passes us in the hallway, and we jump.

"Ahh!"

"What is it with you two?" Maggie says, looking at us oddly. She is 18 and dressed all in black: black jeans, black turtleneck, and bare feet. Her jet-black hair is wet and pulled up in a loose bun, that sits on top of her head. I watch as she takes a quick look back at us to see if we are still freaked out, she then walks the same path my mother did to the kitchen.

"What is going on with them?" we hear Maggie ask my mother.

Then my mother not so subtly looks through the brick pass-through window that peeks out from the kitchen into the family room to check on us. *If that isn't an obvious sign that we're being talked about, I don't know what is.*

"I think they are just playing around," we hear Mom reply; then to us, "Come on girls; your waffles are getting cold."

Emily says, "Come on." I scowl for a minute and let her drag me into the kitchen for breakfast.

I see Maggie already sitting at the kitchen table. The window behind her sends light over her dark hair, almost making it look white in the bright light of day. She prepares to eat my mother's homemade waffles and drops a big glob of maple syrup on them. As I watch, my mind goes over last night's events and I'm suspicious of her all over again, and my anger surges.

Without thinking, I let go of Emily's hand and yell, "We know what you did last night!"

"Oh no!" I hear Emily whisper under her breath as she takes a step back, separating herself from me while covering her mouth with her hand.

"Becca, what are you talking about?" asks my mother, as she walks toward us trying to survey the situation.

I take a step back myself at what I just said. I'm not usually confrontational. *How could I have just blurted that out?* But then I see my sister's face. She looks confused and mean at the same time. She's clearly upset at me for talking to her like that and she looks ready to pounce. Typical moody teenager. Seeing the look on my mother's face sparks my courage and I'm ready to fire back.

"Mom," I start, "last night we heard noises! Very strange, loud sounds coming from the hallway, and I know it was her just trying to scare us! It had to be her! There wasn't anyone else in the house!" Adding one more jab, "She is always so mean!"

My emotions soar through the roof, sending tears to

my eyes, but I try not to cry. I know my mother is upset with me, but I don't really care. I will say it; I will speak up and tell my mother what my sister did. *She has to see it was wrong! You can't treat people like that!* It's not funny, and she can't get away with it.

Maggie has the nerve to make her pretty, freckled face look shocked.

"Sorry, Becca. I don't know what you're talking about." *Now she has the nerve to sound like she feels sorry for me?*

"You two heard noises last night?" she asked us, looking from me to Emily. "What did you hear?"

Emily chimes in, "We heard big bangs from Becca's room, coming from the hallway! It happened the first time around midnight and then again around 4 a.m."

"And you think it was me?" my sister asked, as she lifted her right hand and held it to her chest in confusion.

"Yes." I say sharply, looking her in the eye. "You know you did it! Just admit it! You love to upset me, and it was just a bonus that my friend was here!" I say as I cross my arms over my chest, my face filled with anger.

"Yeah, ok, sure," replies my sister, as she picks up her fork and waits to put her food in her mouth until after she is done speaking to us. "You're right, I do. But sorry to inform you, it couldn't have been me. I came home last night after 2 a.m. and went right to bed. I was so tired I didn't even change my clothes. I didn't want to wake anyone and fell right asleep. So, I'm sorry to tell you, but it couldn't have been me."

"Oh, my God!" Emily gasps, as her mouth falls open listening to my sister's explanation.

"Okay, Okay!" comes my mother's voice. We all

look at her standing near the brick wall in the kitchen directly across from the table. She has her usual *you're getting carried away* look on her face. Suddenly I feel sick.

"No, Mom," I cry to her. "What we are saying is true!" I plea. "I am not making this up and I'm not exaggerating!" My mother always thinks I exaggerate because I love to write stories and journal. "This is real." I look at her trying to get her to listen. "This DID happen last night! Even Emily heard it!"

"Okay," says my mother as she comes closer to me. She gently takes my hands and slowly puts them down at my sides because the more I talk, the more worked up I get, and the more I wave my hands around. "So, you heard something," Mom says. "It could have been the house settling." Then she goes back to the waffle maker, picks up the batter and pours some onto the hot waffle iron.

"Mom!" I plea again. "We checked the hallway and it was dark! That's where the noise came from," I say. "No one was there."

"Yeah," Emily says weighing in. "We did check the hallway, after we heard a big thud several times; and Becca is right. No one was there and the hall was pitch black. No one had been in the bathroom or anything."

"Okay," says my mother. "So, we don't know what it was, but it's probably just like I said – the house settling. When it's cold outside, the house sometimes makes creaky noises. But whatever it was, you are upset over nothing and accusing your sister, which isn't nice. If she says it wasn't her, then it wasn't her. Let it go."

Now I know she doesn't believe me and she's just

trying to put the issue to rest. It's useless to go on.

With a long sigh, I say, "Fine." I feel like I can taste the defeat.

"Okay, then," says my mother as she hugs me. She makes Maggie stand up and then tells us both to hug. Against our will, we do. As I hug my sister, I see my mother smile.

My sister and I release each other from our fake embrace, and she looks at me with a tired expression. Then she takes her seat again at the table. Picking up the *Troy Daily News* from the middle of the kitchen table, Maggie begins flipping through, finding what she's looking for and starts reading. *Ugh. Do I have to read the paper some day? That sounds awfully boring. She is too young for that!*

Emily and I just stare at her as she reads, wondering what just took place, and why we got nowhere telling the truth. Then my mother gives Emily and me a plate.

"Okay, girls," she says. Looking directly at us, she prompts us toward her famous waffles that are being kept hot in the oven in a covered pan. "Time for some waffles!"

My mother dishes out her waffles, pushing us back toward the table to eat. We look at each other and take our seats near my sister. I see our dog get up from where she is and walk over to join us, as she sits near us on the floor getting ready to beg for waffles. Why am I not surprised?

As Emily butters and cuts up her waffles, I watch my sister to see if she is shows any emotion.

Of course she did it, right? I convince myself, as I stare at her while she reads the newspaper. Then she looks over at me. "Want part of the paper?"

"Oh, my God!" I whisper. Understanding hits me.

"What?" Maggie asks, somewhat confused. She continues holding up the paper, offering to pass it to me.

"What is it?" Emily asks, slowly putting down her fork, almost afraid to take another bite.

"She didn't do it."

TRANSFERRED

After dinner, Julia and Tom excused the remaining two children from the table telling them to get ready for bed. "Excused" was an exaggeration – the kids got up and left the dinner table and their parents let them, asking simply that they get ready for bed.

"I want to see you in your pajamas in ten minutes with teeth brushed," Julia called out as they ran out of the dining room, through the small foyer, around the corner, and down the hallway to their bedrooms.

"I mean it!" she warned.

The parents carried the remains of their dinner into the small kitchen and Julia began cleaning up. The couple worked as a team in silence until the chore was done. This was the extent of their togetherness most days.

When the kitchen was clean, Julia turned to her husband and saw that he still looked like the weight of the world was on his shoulders. His dark hair lined his upset brow and pale skin; his eyes had no sparkle in them tonight.

Looking more concerned than Julia had ever seen him, her mind went from a bad day at work thought, to fired from work, to someone dying. That had to be it; someone died.

"We have to talk," said Tom, guiding her to the couch in their formal living room around the corner from the children's hallway and bedrooms. He wanted to be far enough away that the kids couldn't hear their conversation.

"I got some news today at work, which should be good news, but I'm afraid you won't take it as good news," Tom told his wife as he took her hand in his.

Terrified, she wanted to turn away. To run away. If she didn't hear whatever it was he had to say, it wouldn't happen. She was not happy; she had just eaten dinner; she thought she was going to be sick.

"I got called into my boss's office today. Remember Mike Myers?" Tom waited for his wife to nod, and then he moved on. "He said I was doing an amazing job on the Smith contract, and since I was so driven, it was time for another raise and promotion."

"Oh, my God," cried Julia, as she leaped toward her husband, wrapping her arms around his strong neck. "Tom, I am so happy for you! For us! This is the best news!" Julia said enthusiastically. "I know how hard you've been working, and I am so proud of you!" But as she pulled her arms away and got a good look at his face, she noticed his downturned lips, sad eyes, and wrinkled brows. He didn't have the look of someone who was giving his wife great news.

Ahhh, now the part where I may not see it as good news, she thought to herself.

"What is it? Did someone die today, too? You have been so upset since the moment you walked through the door and I don't understand why. I *need* to know." Julia reached out to him and placed her hand on top of his, looking into his eyes with comfort and a bit of concern.

"Julia, with this promotion comes a transfer to Akron, Ohio." Tom couldn't even make eye contact as he told her. "We have to be in Akron by January."

He knew how devastated she would be leaving this town and home she had come to love and adore. Last year, a Catholic priest blessed the house. She had gotten a little giddy about having a huge party with a blessing ceremony. She invited everyone from their church and the entire neighborhood to celebrate their wonderful home. He had never seen her that happy in his life, not even on their wedding day!

"God, Julia, I am so, so sorry!" Tom took his wife's hand and tried to comfort her as he spoke. He used a genuine, soft, and tender voice, as his eyes finally met hers, hoping she would understand that this was painful for him, too.

He knew he was not a great husband because he worked so much. He wanted to make sure she knew that he honestly cared – that he was on her side. He needed her to see he was upset about the transfer… that he didn't want to take her away from all of this. But to not accept the promotion? That was unheard of! He'd outgrown his position in Troy and the whole goal was to work hard and keep moving up the ladder.

Tom wanted to be there for her and maybe, just maybe, this was meant to be. Yes, it would be hard on them both, but maybe, it would bring them closer together.

However, his words had an immediate, negative effect. While Tom spoke with such sweet care, Julia hadn't heard a word. She was in shock.

Tom was still speaking to his wife, almost in tears himself. He felt so bad that he couldn't do anything to stop her pain. He wanted so desperately to keep her in the home she truly loved.

Staring into space, Julia sat in silence.

"Honey?" he spoke to her calmly. "Honey, are you alright?" he said in a low voice. Tom waited for the blow. He waited for his wife to turn on him and start yelling, screaming, and yes, maybe even hitting him, before running away from him. But it never came. She didn't speak. She didn't blink. She didn't move.

Motionless, she just sat there. Tom watched his wife's face and got more worried by the second. Her reaction was worse than he had predicted.

"Honey, I love you. And sweetheart," he soothed as he continued to hold her hand, "I'm so, so, so sorry! I hope you can forgive me someday." Tom spoke from the heart, hoping his wife would look at him and say something. Anything!

Maybe this is my wake-up call, he thought, watching Julia sit in silence, unmoving, staring into space. Yes, this was his wake-up call to be kinder and get closer to her.

"Julia?" Tom spoke again.

"Mom!" Sara yelled, her voice breaking the shock for them both. In a blink of an eye, Julia was back in the world again.

"Hey, honey," said Tom as Julia looked about the room. He began rubbing her back and breathed a sigh of relief as she snapped back to reality.

However, after Julia looked at Tom, she pushed him away, and stood up. She looked around the room once more, trying to take in where she was and what was happening. Blinking a few more times she glanced back at Tom. And walked away.

As he watched her, he retreated back inside himself feeling worse than ever. Tom couldn't speak. He couldn't move. Thinking nothing could make this better.

Does she hate me? Will she ever speak to me again? Tom sat with tears threatening to spill out his eyes as his worst fears swirled around in his mind.

He let the tears spill.

Julia walked in a trance down the hall. Though she couldn't recall her mission, she knew she had one. One of the kids needed something.

"Mom!" called Sara again.

Julia walked into Sara's bedroom and spotted her lying in her bed. The walls were drenched in bright pink paint and Barbie dolls were all over the floor. Julia tripped slightly over all her daughter's My Little Ponies, as she walked toward her daughter. With a sigh, almost breaking into tears, she sat on the edge of Sara's bed. The little girl looked so cute and innocent, as she lay in her pink fluffy sheets and comforter pulled all the way to her chin.

As Julia looked down at her little girl, something inside her died. Just like that. *What do I tell the kids?* It took everything to hold it together and choke back her tears. She needed to protect her daughter from her own ugly emotions. Julia just knew, if she started to cry, she would never stop.

Who Did It?

"I'm confused," Emily states, as we get ready for the day, our bellies full of waffles. She's deep in thought as she packs up her stuff, waiting for her mother to pick her up.

"What did you mean, 'she didn't do it'? How can that be? There wasn't anyone else it could have been. Your mother was sleeping and went to sleep before us; we saw her go into her room. Then your little brother, Zander, is afraid of the dark and was already in bed, before your mom was. That only leaves your sister, who came in late last night," she stresses.

"I know it looks that way; I have to admit. But think about it. If it were her, don't you think she would have said something to me? Don't you think she would have gloated when my mom wasn't looking?" I ask her.

"Huh," she replies, considering what I just said.

"I think she would have made sure I knew it was her last night, to get credit for scaring us."

"Think about it, frightening the two of us! If she had done it, she had the perfect opportunity to tell us at a time when my mother wouldn't hear, she would have," I say to Emily, "but she didn't! Also, she wouldn't have been nice to me and offered me something like the newspaper, if she had scared us. Something is off."

"Yeah!" agrees Emily. "I did think that was weird. She is never nice to you."

"Yep, if it were her, she would have made sure we both knew it last night, and she had the perfect chance to tell us. So it wasn't her. It couldn't have been," I insist, more confident of myself every time I repeat it.

"Plus, she loves it when we're mad and fighting with her over something she's done to scare us," Emily continues, putting on her socks and placing her clothes from last night neatly in her bag.

Finally, dressed in torn jeans and a tie-dyed t-shirt her mother bought for her at a festival, Emily keeps trying to piece together my logic. "So, when Maggie didn't gloat, that's when you knew she wasn't the one who was in the hallway last night?" Her red freckles get brighter against her pale skin when she overthinks. Her long, curly, red hair whips back and forth with the tilt of her head, as she ponders both sides.

"Yeah, that's how I know – it wasn't like her at all," I say, breaking into her thoughts.

"True, but ummm," she continues as she tries to find the right words. She looks over at me with a frightened look on her face, clearly not wanting her thoughts to go in the direction they're headed.

"What?" I panic for a second, looking around the room to see why she's afraid. "What is it?"

"The only thing is," she pauses and looks back at me. "If it wasn't her, or me, or you, or Zander, or your mom, then who was it? Or *WHAT* was making all that racket?"

"Becca?" she finally says to me when I still haven't answered.

I'm scared into silence.

WHAT NOW?

The next morning, Julia woke up to find her husband gone. It was 7 a.m. and she was already crying. After she got the kids ready and off to school, she was finally alone in the house, so she no longer had to try to hide it. She felt too many emotions for her to have any shred of control. And the tears rolled.

Today's going to be just as pathetic as last night.

After putting their daughter to bed last night, Julia poured herself a glass of wine. She'd bought it ages ago, but really wasn't much of a drinker. *Not before last night anyway.* She ended up having more than one glass, while she cried on the floor of their closet.

She felt as if someone had died. Julia mourned the approaching death of her current life. Her heart was broken, and her body ached because of it. She wanted to be like other people and be okay with the move, be supportive of the promotion, go with the flow. But so many feelings were surfacing and pouring out of her. And none of them involved going with the flow.

After crying herself to exhaustion, Julia finally fell asleep on the closet floor. She woke at 4 a.m., walked quietly in the dark to their bed, and softly crawled in, careful not to wake her husband. She hadn't spoken to Tom at all after his announcement for fear of saying something she'd regret. Something hurtful. It was probably best to stay away for now as she was feeling so much hate, resentment, and anger toward him.

MRS. WALTER

"Alice White come on down!" shouts the television host, as a woman in a blue bulky sweater jumps out of her seat with glee, then runs toward the game show host.

"Next," I announce to no one from my front-row seat on the floor in front of the television, as I start flipping through channels with the remote. I want to watch *Roseanne*, my favorite show, but it's not always on this time of day.

As I flip through the channels, I look back to check on Zander. He's only a toddler, so I need to check on him frequently. Thankfully, he's just hanging out on our blue couch by the French doors, probably watching squirrels or chipmunks, or whatever strolls by the window and peeks back at him. But now that I'm flipping channels he seems mesmerized by the television screen regardless of what's playing. *Okay, he's good.* I turn my attention back to mindless flipping.

"Oh, good! *Roseanne!*" *You can't go wrong with this show!*

Another quick glance back at Zander to see if he's cool with me leaving the channel here. Thankfully, he seems content. Sometimes, he throws a fit if cartoons aren't on and it's not worth fighting over, so he just gets his way. Since he's engrossed, I go back to the show and the necklace I'm making. It is just Zander and me at home after school. My sister went to college a month ago in September. I love the quite time, but she worked a lot this past summer, so we have been used to it being 'just us' for a while now.

This is why I like to sit on the floor in front of the television watching reruns. I have a homemade bread-making kit and make jewelry like necklaces and rings. Here on the floor, I can spread out my beads and stuff and not worry about them spilling all over the place

Zander and I have our routine down pat: I get off the school bus at 4 p.m. and walk over to Zander's babysitter's house. Mrs. Martin is super nice and lives in the neighborhood so the walk is no biggie. She used to babysit me, too. I take him off her hands and we make the trek back to our house. Then I'm in charge of Zander until Mom gets home. That's never a set time. Sometimes she doesn't get home until really late because she has three different jobs. That seems like a lot, but she says it's okay.

A few weeks have passed, without a trace of any strange activity in the house, and life has gone back to normal. All the weird, unexplained noises seem forgotten.

Zander and I chill in comfortable silence together for a while. *It's nice,* I think, as I grab a couple more beads to string. But two re-runs of *Roseanne* later, I hear Zander crying from the couch. I spin around to face him and try to figure out what's the problem.

"Zander, what's wrong?"

As I watch him more closely, I see him looking toward the kitchen. It seems like whatever is happening in there is the cause of his distress. He *actually seems terrified!*

I follow his gaze and see that our dog, Gypsy, next to me, is also looking into the kitchen. "What in the …" I say as I see the kitchen lights flickering on and off. As soon as I notice that, I hear the garbage disposal start running.

Grrrr. …Grrrr. … the disposal grinds from the kitchen.

Zander is now screaming louder and louder at the addition of the disposal noise. I don't blame him.

I jump up to get a closer look through an opening near the fireplace. That's when I see her … a short pale woman with short brown, curly hair. Her make-up is so perfectly applied that I can see it from here. She's wearing blue eye shadow with red lipstick, a light pair of blue jeans, and a bright coral sweater.

And she's staring right at me. *Actually, she's* smiling *at me.* I feel stuck, like my feet are frozen in place. My body clearly will not move. *Now she's reaching for a … wait! What the hell is she doing?*

She's making the peanut butter and jelly sandwiches! After Zander and I got home, I grabbed peanut butter, jelly, a knife, and a loaf of bread, and set them on the yellow countertop. Then I was distracted, when Zander needed help getting his shoes off, and forgot all about it. Now, this stranger is standing in front of the countertop with the butter knife in her left hand spreading the jelly over our bread. As she spreads it, she reaches for the Peter Pan peanut butter with her right and glances back at me with another big smile.

WHO IS THIS LADY??

Okay, I have to go put a stop to this, but I am absolutely scared to death and cannot move!

Behind her, I see the refrigerator door is wide open. As I watch her intently, trying to figure out what is happening, it seems as if she is trying to show me how to make a peanut butter and jelly sandwich! Without saying a word, she continues on her mission with a big warm smile on her face.

Suddenly, Zander's screams break my attention and I run around the fireplace into the kitchen and stop.

She's gone.

Where did she go? Just like that, she vanished! I assume she's run around the corner and is hiding somewhere in the house. I need to run after her, but first I take in the scene around me. The kitchen lights are still flashing, and the garbage disposal is still running. When I look over to the switches, I realize they're both moving on their own. As if an invisible force or child were sitting there moving them back and forth to annoy its audience.

First things first. The noise and the lights must be scaring Zander so, if I can get the noise and lights to stop, he may settle down. The kitchen light and garbage disposal switch are on the same switch panel, making it easier for me. I quickly look over at them, then check to see if the strange lady has reappeared. As I stand in the kitchen, I become aware of my poor little brother's screams coming from the other room. With an anger welling inside, I run toward the switches and place my hand on them both, to stop them from moving.

What the heck? I actually *feel* the switches moving under my palm. I'm stunned, irritated, and scared. Then I lift my left hand and use both it and my right, to lean all my body weight on the switches, with as much force as I can, to try to keep them from moving.

Finally, after what feels like an eternity, the switches slow, then stop. The lights and garbage disposal turn off, and the house is silent once more.

Now that I can hear myself think, I turn to scan the kitchen and the family room. I turn around, whip open the garage door and scan the empty garage. No one is there.

I close the door behind me and turn back to my poor little brother, Zander, scared and alone on the couch, tears filling his little red eyes. I run over and pick him up. Pressing him against my body, as tightly as possible, I do my best to comfort him, whispering in his ear that everything will be all right, and that the lady is gone. I say it to comfort him, but *I don't know if that is even true!*

With Zander on one hip, I start walking around the house to see if anything else is amiss. First, I walk into the kitchen where she stood looking at me through the peek-a-boo brick window and survey the mess. I see two pieces of bread with jelly spread on them and two more pieces of bread with large amounts of peanut butter on top. The knife she clearly used is lying right beside them. The jar of creamy Peter Pan peanut butter and bread bag are wide open on the countertop. The refrigerator door is still open, but the light inside is off, probably from being left open for so long.

I'm scared, but I try not to let Zander notice that, as I step toward the sliding door that leads into our dining room.

This must be the way she went. Inching closer to the door, I pull a giant knife from the kitchen's knife rack on the counter ... the one our mother always uses to cut our birthday cakes. It's huge and very long! *This will scare a burglar!*

I quickly shift Zander to my other hip, as I quietly make my way forward, hoping she doesn't hear me.

SHE HATES ME

"She hates me!" Tom yelled out loud, as he kicked a balled-up piece of paper on his office floor that hadn't quite made it into the trash bin. He stood behind his desk in his small white-walled office. He was so frustrated. *Why!!* He thought to himself.

Throwing his body into his desk chair, he went limp and sighed. *How could I do this to her?* Tom placed his forehead in his hands, trying to hold back the tears.

Full of regret and seriously concerned for his wife, Tom tried to call home throughout the day. *Why won't she answer!*

Was she busy? Perhaps, but his guess was that she was still angry at him and wasn't ready to talk. He was especially worried, because of how she acted after he broke the news about his transfer. He remembered her sitting motionless in a weird daze, until she heard Sara's voice. She hadn't had anything to do with him since. Granted, it hadn't been long, but still. Not a glance. Not a touch. Not a word.

He left earlier than normal that morning, just to give her some space. He was too afraid to risk upsetting her further, to start a conversation that early in the morning. So he just left the house.

His remorse was strong, and his thoughts kept going straight to the worst-case scenario. *I should have just refused the offer. Will she divorce me over this?*

Tom began rocking back and forth in his black leather chair, his fingers slowly rubbing his stressed temples as he tried to self-sooth. He was clearly tortured about the unknown whereabouts of his wife. Then he heard a familiar voice.

"Tom?"

Letting go of his head, Tom's hands fell to his lap as he looked up.

"Oh. Hi, Mike," Tom replied to his boss, as he quickly tried to recover. He aimlessly worked at straightening his unusually messy desk. He hadn't exactly paid much attention to it today. Normally, he was neat and tidy, and insanely organized, but today was different.

"Are you alright?" Mike asked, with concern in his voice.

"Yeah. Why wouldn't I be?"

"I don't know. You just seem out of sorts is all."

"I do?" said Tom, as he slumped back into his chair.

"Is there something on your mind? I'm all ears if you need it," Mike said, in a friendly non-boss-like manner.

"Well," Tom tried to muster the courage, to say what no man should say to his boss. He wanted to say, "please promote me and let me stay here with no transfer so my wife will not hate me, and we can live happily ever after! I promise I will do whatever you want and be the best employee you've ever had!" However, he knew he couldn't.

"It's my wife," Tom stated to his boss. As Tom spoke, he felt his whole demeanor shift, becoming a bit emotional. "I'm worried about her. I told her the news about my promotion last night and well, let's just say she didn't take it well."

"I see." Mike responded as he continued to listen.

"Julia REALLY loves it here and I've gotten

transferred so many times now. I think she thought this was it! That maybe this time, it would be the last transfer. She has really settled in. Our neighbors are great, and she's really involved with our church as a volunteer. She is just so happy!"

"So, what are you saying exactly?"

"I don't really know, sir," replied Tom, with sorrow in his deep male voice.

"Are you saying that you don't want to move? That you don't want this promotion?"

"No, sir," replied Tom with haste. "I just didn't expect what should have been good news to be so upsetting to my wife, essentially to our whole family."

"Look, Tom," said his boss, walking closer to the cherry desk and finally taking the nearby chair intended for guests. He sat down in front of Tom, with general concern obviously on his face. "I think as myself not just as your boss, but as your friend. A good friend, I hope."

"You are, Mike. And I appreciate it."

"If you don't take this promotion with the transfer, there will be no more climbing. You have hit the ceiling here." There was an unmistakable seriousness to his voice, as he looked Tom in the eye. "Understand?"

"Oh," replied Tom, in surprise.

"You are literally at the top of the game here. Troy, Ohio, only has so much. The plant in Akron - that's the big plant. That's where bigger things can happen for you!"

Tom was silent for a few moments, just taking in what his boss and friend had laid out. "I guess I did know that, but was hopeful there was a viable Plan B."

"No. There isn't. The only other option is staying. It's your choice. You can take the job in Akron or stay here in Troy. If you stay here, you'll be in this position with limited pay raises until you retire."

Tom looked away from Mike to collect himself and think. He sighed loudly, probably too loudly, as he looked down at his feet and hunched over further in his chair. Then, he took another deep breath and returned to the conversation.

"What am I going to do?" he asked rhetorically. "Julia will hate me for this. I know it. Even though it sounds dramatic, I know it's true! You didn't see her reaction last night. And you're not the one she's shut out." Tom said, turning back toward his boss to face him. "She won't even speak to me or pick up the phone to even hang up on me!"

"Look," spoke Mike, in his buddy voice again, "So she's upset for now, and maybe for a little while longer, but you all will grow from this adventure. You'll adjust to a new location and home, and new life together. Julia will make new friends and find a new church, and all will be well. It might take a while for her to see it, but it will all be okay."

"That's just the thing. She's actually from Akron. She grew up there and her parents are still there." Tom told his friend. "I was hoping she would see the move as positive, but when I told her, she just went cold and distant. She hasn't spoken to me since."

Mike, seeming to have an easy solution for everything, chimed in again, "Okay, she was upset yesterday, and it was a shock, but she's had time to think about it; let it sink in. I'll bet you by the time you get home, Julia will be more receptive to the move."

"I know I have to accept the promotion. Heck, I already have. And don't think I'm not appreciative of the opportunity. I am just trying to keep my family sane at the same time."

"Be open-minded," ensured his boss and friend. "Maybe it'll help her be more open to the idea."

"Oh, God. She's going to just keep hating me." Tom put his forehead back into his hands and again tried to rub away the stress.

SO, I FOLLOWED IT

I feel like I've been down this road before. I stand still, Zander on my hip, listening for any kind of sound as I gesture to him to be quiet. I put a finger to my lips saying, "Shhh … Don't move." He nods his head.

We stand in front of the sliding door where the woman in our house must have gone when she left the kitchen. *Where else would she have gone?* I don't hear a thing and the silence is deafening!

Making a spur of the moment decision, I move forward to protect my house, Zander, and my precious dog, Gypsy, who is with us. She is also frightened after seeing our reaction to the lights and garbage disposal. Filled with a fresh rush of adrenaline and a strong urge to fight, I press on.

Walking slowly through the small sliding doorway, I step into the next room. I take a fast look around the small dining room, which is basked in the sunlight coming from the large window on the side of the house. Our glass dining room table and steel chairs are the only furnishings in the room. There are no decorations or knick-knacks. We simply can't afford them. Everything we have is left over from my parent's home before the divorce and move. My mother didn't buy anything for the house, except paint.

I don't see anyone.

I stand silently, near the door for a moment, then

look behind us to see if anyone has reappeared in the kitchen. No one. *She must be around the corner or in Mom's bedroom.*

I tell Zander to be silent once more and give Gypsy a tug on her collar as I move forward. *Holding the large knife in my hand would be so much easier if I weren't carrying another human on my hip.* Rounding the bend where my mother's bedroom meets the hallway, I inch forward into her bedroom as I try not to make a sound. *I'm not even sure I am breathing.* I don't see her. *Yet.* I keep going until I'm on the far side of my mother's bed. By now, I'm moving purely by fear and anger. *I must find her!* I peek over the bed and see nothing, so I bend down and pull up the king-sized bed skirt to peek underneath.

But there's no one there. No one hiding in the curtains or under or behind my mother's furniture either! *How could this be?*

"Okay," I whisper to my little brother, as I re-hike him up my small hip. He's starting to look a little bored and has completely lost interest in what is happening. He probably thinks we're just playing some sort of hide-and-seek. I'm thankful for his three -year-old logic.

One more spot in here. *I think I may throw up.* I'm too afraid to set Zander down, but when I think about it, carrying him into every scary situation as I search for the intruder in the house doesn't seem like a good idea either. I just don't want him hurt! If I put him down somewhere for me to look around, that strange woman could snatch him up and take off with him. I would never see him again. *So here we go,* I think as we walk into my mom's bathroom and closet. There certainly is nowhere else for this woman to go. She has to be in here. And she can't escape without going past me now.

Grabbing my dog's collar once again, I tug her along while I have the knife sticking straight out, as if I'm ready to skewer someone, the other hand holding Zander. Fear still rushing through my body, I release the dog and I turn to flick on the light over my mother's white porcelain sink. A quick scan reveals she is not there, which only leaves the closet. *Crap!*

Putting my little brother into the bathtub, I gesture, *shhhh...* to him again, then quickly whip open the door and turn on the closet light as fast as I can.

"Aghhh!" I scream from adrenaline and fear. *I can't take it anymore!*

No one is there.

Just wanting this over with, I grip the knife in one hand as I repeatedly punch the hanging clothes in the closet with the other. If she's in here, I'll hit her eventually!

"COME OUT!" I scream as loudly as I can as hate fills my voice. "I've had enough! Who are you? Why are you in my house?" I keep checking through the clothes. *I have never been this mad!*

"Stay here," I say to my brother, a little too snippy, then whip the shower curtain closed, so he doesn't think to get out of the tub. He's probably safer there, than with me holding a knife.

I make a mad dash out into the hallway and through the foyer to check the three deadlocks in our front door. The locks all require a key to get in or even out of the house. They're all locked. *How did she get in?*

I continue to run through the rest of the house searching. While I'm not lugging around another person, it sure is easier to search. No one is behind any of the furniture in the living room. No one is in my brother's new room, which used to be my sister's until she went to college. No one is under his bed or in his closet. The only bedroom I haven't checked is my own!

Jumping to my feet, I take off toward my room. I run in and stop near the end of my bed. I quickly lift my comforter almost tearing it off my bed in my hurry to check under it.

Nada. No one under the bed, or behind the door, or in the closet. I checked it all. No one is there.

Oh no, our bathroom! It's the only place I haven't checked in the whole house! Now hesitant, I take small and quiet steps forward, proceeding to the bathroom that my little brother and I share located at the end of the long hallway.

I slowly pick up my right foot, setting it back down on the off-white ceramic floor in our bathroom. The last place I could possibly check! Taking a deep breath, I listen intently for any movement at all. I peek behind the dark brown wooden door and don't find anyone. I can see the rest of the bathroom and see no one. However, someone could be hiding behind the bathtub curtain. We have a thick plastic dark pink shower curtain, with white and blue large flowers printed on it to match our blue and white bathroom. When you are in the shower, you can't even see out. If someone walks in when you are in the shower, you can't see them.

Quietly, I begin taking steps closer to the shower curtain, the intensity in me rising. *WHO IS THIS WOMAN AND WHY IS SHE IN MY HOUSE?!*

As I inch closer, the curtain's flowers seem to taunt me, as if they are trying to make me feel peaceful and happy with its pretty design. But my mind is filled with questions, fear, and a bit of rage. I don't want to be taken off guard by someone hiding behind it! Slowly, I lift my right hand, reaching across my own body and grab the edge of the shower curtain in the middle, as it hangs to the floor. Taking one more step forward, I am now in line with our pale-blue tub. I take in a deep breath for confidence and listen again for movement behind the bathroom's shower curtain. It's still silence that fills me with hostility and I suddenly whip open the shower curtain expecting to confront my enemy, but .... Nothing!

How can this be?

Julia Packs Up the House

It's December and there were only a few weeks left to spend in her precious home until she must leave. The real estate agent sold their home in record time. Only one week on the market. Obviously, the new family could see how wonderful it was. Why wouldn't they want such a great house?

Julia wondered if things would ever be the same. In the last few weeks, they had told the children about the move and dealt with all their wild emotions. She simply didn't speak to Tom unless she had to; he slept on the couch most nights because Julia would tell him she needed the lights on to stay up late to pack. Their relationship had really taken a turn for the worse. Julia tried, but she couldn't let go of her anger.

This was the only home she ever loved and wanted to be here forever. She loved the neighbors; the kids had friends to play with next door. She finally was the most favored volunteer at St. Patrick's, their Catholic church in Troy, and she was so happy. Tom's transfer here felt right, like home. Sure, her family treated her badly, ignored her, and neglected her, but her outside life made up for it. She was happy, enough that she just pretended those bad things didn't matter. Pretended they didn't happen. And pretended they didn't hurt.

However, in the past few weeks, her older son, Kyle, was acting out in negative ways. At school, he had cut class by telling the teacher he was going to the bathroom only to pull the fire alarm. He was caught and the police were called. The school filed a police report and he was suspended.

Julia dealt with the situation. She met the police officers, who were called about the incident, and the principal in his office. As soon as Julia began speaking to her son about what happened, he began belittling her in front of everyone. The officers shook their heads in disbelief as her son got up and walked out of the principal's office, out of the school, and out to his mother's car, where he waited impatiently for her.

In the next few weeks, he was given a massive amount of homework from teachers to try to salvage the year before the move. He refused to do it and if Julia mentioned it, he cursed at her and left the house, not coming home until after dark. When he did finally come home, he would walk into the house and go directly to his room without speaking to anyone. When he was home, Tom also tried to talk to Kyle, but Tom's travel schedule kept him busy much of the time.

It was sad how little control they had.

Julia felt it was no use. *I might as well give up,* she thought to herself. As the moving date in January got closer, Julia seemed to have shut much of the world out. She kept to herself and packed. Mostly she reminisced. She picked up so many of her favorite treasures and let her mind wonder. Then she would start the whole cycle again: sleep, get up, dress, clean, prepare the boxes Tom had picked up for their move, and pack.

The packing was emotionally exhausting. You could just throw things in a box, but there was the paper, the taping, and choosing the right size box for items. It was so tedious! And then there was the labeling – if she didn't label the boxes, it'd take even longer for them to find out which boxes went where once they got to the new place. *The new place.*

Julia took some moments to herself, during the seemingly endless packing, to stop and look around. She remembered being in their previous home packing this stuff up to move here. She was unsure about Troy and hated moving again but told herself she had to support her husband. Tom told her how great this town would be, and the street looked so nice. They met the Davises across the street while looking at the house and taking measurements. The kids were in the car kicking and screaming at each other while the two couples talked on the lawn, excited for their future in Troy.

Julia also remembered unpacking boxes and trying to find places for everything. She remembered finally taking the time to give things a permanent place in the home. She felt the house open up to her as she sang and danced along with the radio while she was unpacking their things. She could feel the home's love for her, it relished in her warm embrace. It was as if the house could feel her love for it. The house wanted her here and she wanted to live here forever.

But here she was packing up the same belongings to move – again. This time it was different. This time she didn't want to leave. She loved Troy and she knew the house didn't want her to leave either. How could she possibly leave? The other houses weren't really important to her, but this one was different, she felt this was her REAL HOME.

As she was packing the *Home Sweet Home* wooden sign that hung on their front door, a heavy weight pressed on her chest and she suddenly felt like she couldn't breathe. The air was too thick and heavy. As Julia mourned her loss, she caught her breath just enough to begin to cry tears of utter sorrow, from deep down inside. Her sense of loss was overwhelming. The pain was like a twisting knife that tore through her chest, ripping through her heart and torturing her emotions with its sharp blade. She soon gave into its plea and stretched out on the floor next to her half-packed boxes, letting her pain escape.

JULIA'S PACKING OBSESSION

Tom would come home and find Julia packing and crying over the top of a box. He tried to talk with her, but she wouldn't even acknowledge his attempts, acting as if he wasn't even there.

Tom noticed that his wife had become obsessed with packing and cleaning. He knew there was a lot of work to be done, but she seemed to be taking an extraordinarily long time to pull stuff together. One night when he came home, he found the same situation taking place, but something was missing: the smell of dinner. He had worked that night a little later than normal due to closing some client cases before he left. He filed paperwork in the correct place for the next person to find, and he had to train his replacement. As soon as he felt he was ahead, he would find something else he had to do before his last day.

Tom turned to his daughter, Sara, who had just come up to him. "Hi, honey!" he said to his daughter as he wrapped her in a hug, both of them aware of Julia's odd presence.

Julia sat nearby in front of the fireplace on the floor with bubble wrap in her hands crying. Her tears splashed down onto the box she had been packing.

"Hey, sweetheart. Did you eat anything tonight?" he asked Sara, as they both ignored the scene in front of them.

"No," she told her father. "Unless we make something ourselves, we don't eat much these days."

"What?" Tom said, with confusion.

"Mom's been like this for a while. When we talk to her she doesn't even answer us or look at us."

"Are you hungry? When is the last time you ate something?"

"Well, I made Thomas and me a peanut butter sandwich after we got home from school. I asked mom over and over again, but she wouldn't answer me, so I just got the stuff out and did it myself."

"That was nice of you to help him, thank you" responded Tom. He didn't want to upset or scare his daughter, so he just kept his thoughts to himself. "Let's check out what we can have for dinner."

Tom glanced toward Julia again from the corner of his eye so his daughter wouldn't see. Then he led Sara away from her mother and into the kitchen to look for something he could whip up to feed his kids.

TELLING MOM

I wake up and rub my bloodshot eyes. I'm so tired. The footsteps in the hallway increased throughout the night and I was too terrified to sleep. And I wasn't about to get up and look. I'm tired of chasing the unknown.

Unfortunately, my mother is on the other side of the house, so I can't call for her; she won't hear me. If I attempt to go get her, I'll have to walk the dark, scary hallway, and I'm definitely not doing that.

Dragging myself out of bed, I take my shower and get ready for school. I'll only see my mother for a little bit before leaving, so I have to prepare myself to talk with her about what I saw. I have little faith she'll listen to me, but I have to try. She worked last night, so I didn't get a chance to tell her after she got home. It was just too late, we had to eat then hurry up and get ready for bed because it was a school night. So now is my chance.

I walk down the dimly lit hallway wishing, not for the first time, that there was at least a little nightlight or something on. My mother is all about saving electricity so she wouldn't put on the overhead hallway light during the day. In fact, the only time there's a fragment of light in the hallway is from the family room's French doors in the back of the house.

As I move down the hall, I feel a rush of cool air

brush past my forearms. "Brrr ..." I mutter under my breath, and I pick up my pace to get to the kitchen where it's warmer. My sleeves are rolled up, so I pull those down in my rush through the hallway.

Practically running into the kitchen, I see my mother sitting at our kitchen table eating a chocolate Entenmann's donut over her morning *Washington Post*.

"Yay, my favorite!" I cry, as my mother sees my excitement and pushes them towards me.

"I know," she smiles as she pushes the long white donut box toward me. I reach in quickly and stuff my mouth full of donut. Then I think about how to begin this conversation. *Chew slower,* I think to myself. The donut at least gives me some more time.

"Mom," I say, after I swallowed my first bit of chocolaty goodness. "Um, there is something I need to tell you."

"What is it?"

"Well, yesterday I was making my bead bracelets in front of the television when Zander started crying. Okay, I know this is going to sound crazy, but when I looked up, I saw a lady with short brown hair and blue eyes in our kitchen. She smiled at me and she looked like she was making us sandwiches. I had left out bread and stuff to make peanut butter and jelly but forgot about it while I was helping Zander. She was standing right there!" I said, as I gestured toward the counter.

"And the lights and garbage disposal were going on and off like crazy! I thought it was a burglar, but when I went into the kitchen she was gone. Then I had to get the garbage disposal to shut off because it was scaring the daylights out of Zander, and it was really hard getting the light switches to stop moving. They just kept going! It took both hands and all my weight leaning on the switches to get them to stop. I was freaked out and really thought it must be a burglar! So I grabbed your big knife and went around the house in search of the lady. But I never found her."

"And I've been hearing footsteps in the hallway and when I look out, no one is there! Since it's only Zander, you, and me now, since Maggie is at college, it's really freaking me out. I don't understand what it could be, but I can't sleep at night because I'm so afraid."

Phew, I got it all out and it's done. I said it. She's just staring at me. *She's going to commit me to a crazy place where they put me in some straight jacket like a bad horror movie.*

"Becca," my mother finally speaks, as she takes my hand in hers.

Breathing a sigh of relief, I let it out slowly. It's always a good sign when she takes my hands. *She understands and she will tell me what it is or what we can do, and everything will be fine.* I will no longer be afraid of my own house.

"I think you've read too many of those R.L. Stine books you love so much. You always have had quite an imagination," she says, then let's go of my hand and gets up and walks to the kitchen counter to put her dishes in the sink, like nothing has happened.

"But, Mom!" I cry before she turns to leave the room.

"Now, Becca, that's enough!" Mom put her hand up to me in a *stop* motion. "I know you have a very active imagination. You have ever since you were a little girl, but we don't talk about ghosts. We don't believe in that. We are Catholic and we know all that haunted stuff isn't real. Ghosts are for Halloween. That's all. Now, we're going to leave it at that!" Her serious voice tells me we're done with the subject.

And with that, I was never allowed to speak of it again.

Buying and Losing

"I think it's a great house," Tom said, as he, Julia, and the kids got into the car and put on their seat belts. They had just finished looking at a little white house in Akron. It was somewhat of a fixer-upper, but Tom was positive about it. "I know it needs a little bit of work in some of the bathrooms and some heavy cleaning, but I could ask your Dad for help," Tom told Julia, as he watched her expression.

Julia sighed as she put on her seatbelt. Tom and the kids somehow snapped her out of her sad state before heading to Akron for the day. Tom called a local real estate agent and made an appointment to view homes in their price range.

Julia was trying to be positive but felt like she couldn't hold onto it for long. She sighed with a deep sadness and looked ahead as Tom spoke to them in the car.

"Julia?" asked Tom. "The agent says it's a great buy!"

Julia turned to her husband with a half-smile and hard-to-read expression. She was trying and knew he was trying too, but it was strained at best. He contacted the real estate agent completely on his own, which would have normally been her job, so that was good. He was stepping up and trying. But to Julia, the town just didn't feel like home – like it did in Troy. That's all there was to it. She hated growing up in Akron and her feelings hadn't changed. She liked the thought of being closer to her parents, but it didn't outweigh leaving Troy.

Holding back tears she replied, "It's alright, I guess."

"What do you think, kids?" Tom asked the children sitting in the back seat, while he turned slightly, and gave them a thumbs-up, slightly eyeing their mother, as if to say, "Be positive, she can hear you."

"Oh, I liked it! My room seemed nice and big," chimed Sarah.

"Yeah, it sure was!" replied Kyle, with a glare to his sister. "Your room was the biggest room in the house!"

"Kyle!" Tom said, as he looked back and forth between his son in the backseat and Julia up front. He gave Kyle a stern look and raised a brow that at least cooled him off for now.

"Oh ..." began Kyle, after seeing his father's gaze and reaction. "Oh, yeah, I liked the house and my room will be just fine. Don't worry, Mom and Dad."

"Now that is much better."

"Thomas?" Tom said, tapping his four-year-old son on the knee, who also sat in the backseat. Thomas was playing with his robot toys and not paying much attention.

"What?" asked Thomas when he pulled his eyes away from his new red robot.

"What do you think?" asked Tom.

"I think I liked it," said Thomas, in a sweet voice.

"See, the kids are good, which is rare," said Tom to his wife as he gave an awkward half-smile. He was trying to remain positive. "Come on, honey," he said, as he reached over and gave her knee a small love tap. "Maybe this is the house for us! Perhaps this move won't be so bad after all." Tom said to his wife as he looked into her eyes, giving her chin a small chuck with his index finger and putting on his best smile. "Come on, let's be positive."

****

A few weeks later, Tom and Julia closed on a house. Julia wasn't 100 percent satisfied, but she gave up caring. She felt it was pointless to care because life was getting more miserable each day. How could she move on with her life and be happy like everyone kept telling her to do when she wasn't happy, and she only wanted to lie in bed and cry? Meanwhile, Tom brought her flowers every week and tried hard to make her happy. He gave her more hugs and attention, held her hand more in public. He even got a babysitter one night so he could take her out to her favorite restaurant, La Piazza. But when he started talking about the big move during dinner, Julia broke down and had to excuse herself to the ladies' room to pull herself together.

Later that night, after Tom and Julia arrived home and paid the sitter, Tom went right to bed, claiming to be very tired. Julia understood his stress so didn't say anything and let him disappear into their room for the night. She walked to the kitchen and opened a new bottle of wine from Kroger. Looking down at the counter, she saw a note that looked like it was from the children's school. It was from Sara's teacher and she wanted to see her about possible behavior issues in class. *Why don't they just say what they want in the letter? Just come out and say, "This is what your child's problem is and this is how you are going to solve it," and just get it over with!* After a few hours of sitting in the dark as her family slept, Julia finally decided at 1 a.m. to clean things up and head to bed, checking on the kids as she went. Julia walked down the dark hallway to the kids' rooms. Thomas and Kyle shared the first bedroom on the right. She slowly turned the knob and pushed the door open quietly. She saw them both tucked in their beds, safe and sound. Julia stood in the doorway and gazed at her two young children. *Aren't they so peaceful when they're sleeping?* Julia let out a sigh. I wish Kyle were always this quiet. *Why is my life always so hard?* She thought to herself, her body slumping against the bedroom door's wooden frame. *Maybe I'm just selfish? Am I being selfish? I wonder if other women feel this way, that it's just TOO HARD, or is it just me?* Then, a morbid thought popped into her head. *Would they be better off without me?*

MRS. MARTIN

On my way to pick up Zander from Mrs. Martin's on Thornwood Drive, like I do every day after school, my mind is still on what I experienced the other day. *Who was that woman in our house?*

I walk slowly down the long neighborhood street as it curves and bends; eventually Thornwood ends in a cul-de-sac right in front of the babysitter's house, which is about a ten-minute walk from our house. It's an unusually warm day in October, as the sun beats down on my neck and back. I start to sweat and pick up my pace. Maybe it's the heat, but all I can think about are the recent strange events I have witnessed in my home. I keep trying to think of some kind of explanation for what or who I saw, but I just can't. My mind draws a blank every time, which keeps frustrating me. I can't seem to find a sensible reason.

I bring my hands to my eyes and begin to rub them hard. Then, my fingers move to my temples. I'm so stressed and feeling quite overwhelmed, not to mention being scared of my own house! Not being allowed to talk about it doesn't help. *Everyone thinking I am crazy, certainly doesn't make me want to discuss it either.* I can't help but feel forced into a strange silence and it makes me feel SO ALONE.

I wish someone could put their arms around me and tell it is all going to be okay, but I know that without being able to talk to someone about it, that's unlikely.

I wish I knew the truth about what happened in my house that day. Who the woman was, why she was making us sandwiches? Why was she there? And of course, how did she escape without a trace? How could I have not seen her at least once, in all that time I looked for her in the house? It's just not possible!

When I reach Mrs. Martin's house, I walk up the long driveway to the two-story home with its cream siding, brick exterior and green shutters. I walk straight into Mrs. Martin's side garage. I can't help but notice the grass is still green, even though it was a terribly hot and dry summer. They must be watering. Most of their neighbors' lawns are brown and dead.

Inside the garage, I walk over to the two small cement stairs on the right side, laid by Mr. Martin himself, who built the house, and I walk up the steps. Opening the door, I step into the Martins's laundry room and shut the door behind me. I call out to Mrs. Martin like I do every day, "Mrs. Martin, I'm here!" letting her know I'm in the house and then I head into the connecting kitchen where I'm certain I'll find her.

Mrs. Martin has about eleven children that she watches daily and there are even more if school is canceled or it's a holiday that parents don't typically have off work. She's always insanely busy!

As I walk in, I take a deep breath and let out a long sigh. Even though I am now in a busy house full of kids playing, screaming as they go, I still feel helpless and alone. It's hard when no one believes me.

"Hi, Becca!" Mrs. Martin greets me as always. I pull out a stool from under the large kitchen counter and sit.

She doesn't even call for my brother to let him know

that I am there because she knows I won't leave for a while. She knows that I don't like to go home to an empty house. Normally, I stay until after all the other kids are picked up by their parents and her two older children, Madison and Eric, are home from their school or work.

I'm sure Mrs. Martin feels sorry for me. It's not unusual for her to get Zander and me something to eat with her children until her husband, John, gets home from work. But I stay as long as I can most days. It feels nice in their home and I like to be with their family. *Today is definitely a day I will stay as long as I can!*

"Are you okay, girl?" Mrs. Martin asks me when she sees my glum expression. She always emphasizes the word "girl" and sounds like she grew up in the south, even though she was born and raised right here in Troy.

"Yeah, I guess," I reply, as I rest the palm of my hand against my cheek. She looks at me with an odd half smile.

"Umm-hmm," she lets out under her breath. "You sure you're feelin' alright?"

I nod my head and she just looks at me with her half-smile again and repeats her, "umm-hmm."

An hour later, I hop off the stool and walk into the family room to check on Zander, to see if he needs a new diaper. After changing him and packing up his things, I try to convince him to come into the kitchen with me when I hear Mrs. Martin yell at her youngest son, Jordan.

What did he do now? I plop Zander on my right hip and walk into the kitchen. There stands Jordan, covered in Oreo cookie crumbs. He's clearly eaten a cookie from the cookie jar without asking, while his mother prepared dinner right beside him. He's always thinking of sneaky ways to get them. And if you ask him, he'll proudly tell you how good he is at being sneaky! However, the truth is he's not that good. He always gets caught.

"Well, I'll be!" says his mother, as she looks at her son still chewing up the evidence and even popping a second Oreo into his small mouth. "I hope you feel real proud of yourself! You just earned yourself a time out, boy! Now you just march yourself right over to your time out chair! Go on now! Go on!"

As usual, Jordan looks at me with no embarrassment and just smiles as he walks over to his chair of shame, an old-fashioned wooden spindled chair in the far corner of the room. He sits down looking quite pleased. And obviously quite satisfied.

Looking up at his mother who held a wet wooden spoon in her hand, he listens to her lecture. He knew it was coming. Mrs. Martin tells him to sit there for ten minutes and think about what he has done. He keeps on smiling his evil little grin. Trouble is, he looks so cute. Throw in his oversized cheeks, big dimples, tan face, and blue eyes, and he gets anything he wants!

"Jordan! I just don't know what to do with ya! I swear you are a little devil!" she says, addressing her small son, as he continues to smile up at her … still licking the left-over cookie crumbs from his lips.

Jordan looks around his mother at me. He is always getting into trouble and he loves it! I'm not sure if it's the attention he likes or the fact that he just loves being bad.

"Now, Becca," Mrs. Martin starts, speaking as she walks past me to go back to her stew cooking on the stove top. "How was school today? You are awfully silent."

"Fine, I guess." I reply, trying to recall my day at school. *Gosh, what actually happened today?* I've been so busy thinking and worrying about my bad experiences at home and how upset I have been with my mother that I can hardly recall.

"We had pizza!" I yell enthusiastically, happy to remember some aspect of my day. *It's not much, but at least I remembered something.*

"You seem out of sorts. Is everything okay?"

"Sure. Why?"

"Just seems like something is on your mind. You want to talk about it?"

"No."

"Well, alright, but if you change your mind, I am a good listener," she gently informs me.

"Well, the thing is, I really don't know what it is. Or how to explain it." I blurt out. "My mom told me not to talk about it."

Mrs. Martin looks at me a bit and then she looks over at Jordan, who of course, is listening. "Okay, Jordan! You can go play now," she informs him, hinting for him to leave the room.

"That was fast!" he says, and is gone in a flash, running toward the basement yanking open the white glossy door, and racing down the stairs to his toy collection.

"I don't know why I even bother with his time outs," she tells me. "He's just going to keep on being rotten! Nothin' I can do I suppose! Though, I keep trying!

"Okay, I've known you long enough to know when something is bothering you. And it is. Now let's get the cat out of the bag!" She says, looking directly into my eyes and throwing down the dish towel that's been laying nicely on her left shoulder all this time. "I am not sure what your mother said or what's going on, but if you have a problem or had a fight with your mother, maybe I can help."

Mrs. Martin has always been the person I go to if I have a problem or need to talk. Sometimes if I feel like I can't ask my mom something, I'll ask Mrs. Martin.

Mrs. Martin slowly reaches across the large kitchen counter toward me, puts her hand over mine, and looks at me. She has a big heart and I can see in her eyes she wants to help me.

But can she this time?

****

As I pour out my story to Mrs. Martin, telling her about what happened the other day in my house, I hardly pay attention to her reaction. The words just come rushing out of my mouth, like I can't get it out fast enough. I hardly take in a breath while speaking; I'm in such a rush. I tell her everything, talking faster and faster as the story unfolds. As I get to the end of my story about finding every room and closet empty and never finding the woman in my house, I then tell her about how my mother refuses to listen to what I have to say. And I end with my mother telling me that ghosts are only for Halloween and how confused I am over the whole event. I'm breathless and feel like I've rambled on forever. Then I suddenly realize she hasn't said anything yet. When I look up to see Mrs. Martin's face, she's very pale and her jaw is hanging wide open. She looks like *she's* seen a ghost. "Mrs. Martin, are you okay?" I asked getting worried. Pulling herself up and off the counter she was leaning on, I notice she's very pale. She stays quiet, choosing her words carefully. Her face is very serious. I have never seen her this serious before. "Becca, what …" she pauses and closes her eyes for a second, as if summoning the strength to finish the question. "What did this woman look like?" "She was short with brown curly hair and bright blue eyes. And her make-up was perfectly done. Like flawless… Why?" Mrs. Martin gasps. Her eyes pop wide open, as if they might come right out of her head. She raises both her hands to her face, covering her mouth in shock. "What? What's wrong?" I plea. "Becca, you saw Mrs. Walter!"

THE PAIN GETS STRONGER

Once she started crying, it took a long time to stop. She would cry as she wrapped objects in newspaper and bubble wrap, even as she placed them safely into boxes. Tom and the kids, if nearby, would just watch. They learned if they tried to talk to her, she would just ignore their attempts at comforting words.

Julia had heard their words of comfort in the past and just thought they were being nice, because they didn't know what to do with her. Then as time went on and the pain in her heart grew even stronger, their words faded until she no longer recognized their comfort. So, when her kids and husband spoke, she only heard sorrow. It only left her feeling bitter and angry. Soon Julia started to think they were lying to her and that no one really cared about her at all.

Look at everything I have done for all of you! All the meals I have cooked. All the time I spent at your schools volunteering. All the lunches and birthday treats I took to your classmates. The sports activities and everything that came with that! Then there were the Girl Scouts and Boy Scouts and taking you to your troop meetings and events and sales! All the fundraising I did! And let's not forget all the school field trips and birthday parties! And don't forget Christmas and Easter! All for nothing! Julia's thoughts came rapid-fire, angrier by the minute. *Oh, yeah, you really care about me. Care enough about me to move! Like you couldn't help it!*

I won't ever be happy again!

WHO?

"Who?"

"It's Julia Walter," Mrs. Martin repeats, as she looks at me. Her face is white with shock at the realization. "She lived in your house before you," Mrs. Martin explains.

"She had three children and shortly after they moved out of the house, she killed herself in Akron. She and her family just moved there because her husband got transferred for work. I heard she was terribly upset about having to move and she hung herself in their new garage."

"Oh, my God …" I say, as my mouth opens in horror. "That can't be true."

"She used to go to our church actually, St. Patrick's!"

"What! She went to our church, too? This is crazy!" I say to Mrs. Martin, as I begin to rub my head again, just like I did on my way to her house earlier. I'm leaning my elbows on her countertop and barely sitting with my bottom on the edge of the kitchen stool. *This can't be happening!*

"I was in CHRP (Christ Renews His Parish) group with her, back when it started at church. She was so nice. She was just as you described her. She was short with curly, short brown hair, and had bright blue eyes. And when she wore makeup, it was blue eye shadow and always red lipstick," says Mrs. Martin.

"Oh, my God! When I saw her, she was wearing that *exact* makeup: blue eye shadow and red lipstick; and I mean *real* red lipstick."

"Yes!" replies Mrs. Martin with confidence. "That's what she wore to church! Actually, she was a very spiritual woman."

"Really?"

"Oh, yes!" Mrs. Martin replies with enthusiasm. "She even had her house, which is now yours, blessed!"

"Huh?" I ask, never hearing of such a thing before.

"See, she loved that house so much that she had it blessed by a priest," Mrs. Martin's voice is clear with wonderment over her own remembrance of the past.

"Yes, I remember it now. It's been awhile, but yes, she had the priest come and he went around the house with holy water and incense and said a blessing in every room. John and I were there. I remember the priest conducting most of the blessing in front of the brick fireplace. She had a huge party for the blessing and invited everyone at church and half the neighborhood. She even made a huge cake!"

I try to make sense of what I'm hearing, but it's so strange. "This is just too hard to believe," I reply.

"I bet it is. I haven't thought about her in years. But yeah, she loved that house and I think being forced to move was the beginning of her end."

"I can't believe she had the house blessed and she went to our church," I reply, my voice higher than normal, mostly talking to myself.

"Come to think of it, I do remember a time at church when she told everyone after Mass one day that they were moving,"

"Oh, really…"

"We were all very surprised. We knew how much she

loved the house and loved living in Troy, so it was quite shocking to hear they were moving again. Julia told us that she didn't want to move, but that her husband, Tom, had been transferred to Akron. I think she wanted us to know because we had all become friends. And I don't remember her coming back after that," Mrs. Martin continues.

"Geez … how sad," I respond back to her, as I look down at the floor at the thought of how Julia Walter must have felt. "I can't imagine."

"I know," responds Mrs. Martin. "Unfortunately, that was the last time I ever saw her."

"Oh,"

"Yeah." Mrs. Martin looks off into space. "I read in the paper a few months later that she had died and then heard from a neighbor on your street what had happened. It was just unbelievable. Terrible really. She was such a sweet woman."

"Wait, if she went to our church, did my mother know her?"

"No, that was before your parents' divorce and your mother wasn't a part of CHRP yet. It was before she really got involved in the church, so I don't think they would have known each other."

"Oh," I then look back down at the cream laminate floor, my feet dangling off her light wooden kitchen stool now.

"Wow, honey …" Mrs. Martin says, as she walks around the large kitchen counter toward me. She lifts up her arms and wraps them around me in a much-needed hug.

The weight of the conversation is overwhelming. Soon, a heavier sadness sets in. But I'm not sure it's mine. A sudden feeling of deep pain, sorrow, and heartbreak from having to leave the *ONLY* home she ever loved came over me. Then a strong presence of a dark emptiness follows, hitting me like an ocean wave in the face. The kind of wave that knocks you down and you struggle to find the surface to come up for air. The overwhelming emotions are too strong and draining, leaving me feel as if I can barely breathe.

As Mrs. Martin holds me in a tight embrace, my own sad realization comes forth. I always feel strange in my home, but never understand why! Like there's always an unknown or unseen presence. Obviously, I've been living in a home with someone I can't really see!

Could Julia Walter be stuck in our home and can't escape? Is my house her own created hell because Catholic's believe if you commit suicide you go to hell? Could she possibly be stuck in my house for eternity? Is my house truly someone else's HELL??

I want to help, but I know I can't! My mother won't help, so now what?! My Mom told me I could never speak of it again.

An abrupt cry of emotion escapes my heart and I cry out, "Why is this happening?"

"Just let it out, honey," Mrs. Martin tells me in her continued embrace. "Just let it all out."

And I start to cry.

MOVING DAY

The unfortunate day had come for Julia Walter. It was January 5, 1987: moving day.

The moving van arrived early, and Julia was forced out of bed before 7 a.m., which made a bad day even worse. She wasn't happy for many reasons, most of which were because she didn't want to go at all, but now she was losing sleep and unable to savor the few last moments of cozy comfort in her own bed.

"Just my luck," she woke up saying. Tom gave her a strange look, like she was crazy for waking up saying such things.

"Honey, maybe we could look at this day more positively," he told her, with a hopeful smile. "You know, like we're moving on to bigger and better things!" he stated, as he made a fist with his right arm and moved it upward in a "go get'em" gesture.

"Sure," she replied gruffly. "Not today, Tom." Julia continued putting on her slippers then stood up, as she reached for her robe. *This is the last morning I will have in my house. To be where I WANT to be…in Troy.* Julia took a long look around their bedroom. And sighed.

"What is it?" asked Tom, as he watched his wife look oddly around the room.

"This is it," she told him. "This is the last morning in this house," Julia replied, letting out a deep sorrowful sigh once more. She knew it was coming and should have expected it at any given time … but then a tear escaped and quickly made its way down her cheek. *It's early in the morning and I'm already in tears.* Julia looked down at her feet, as if watching her world shatter in that one, single drop. Her head hung in pain, until a loud noise interrupted her thoughts.

Bang, Bang!! The abrupt sound came from the moving van, as one of the movers got out and slid the ramp out the back of the trucks and dropped the end he was holding to the cold ground.

The moving men made their way to the front door and rang the bell. Julia and Tom went to the door and greeted the men who would carry the belongings and boxes that summed up their lives.

It was January, so the air was cold, but at least it had only snowed enough the night before to barely cover the ground. Julia was not looking forward to heavy snow being on the ground. It would just make the move even worse, so at least she had the weather to be grateful for.

The house had taken longer to pack up then they had originally thought, even with Julia doing all that extra pre-packing! But soon the couple, along with their three children were waving goodbye to the men, as the moving van pulled away from their house. The plan was for the men and the van to meet the family at their new house in Akron the next day.

Julia watched the moving van pull away from 2095… her heart reaching out to it as it drove away. She wanted to call it back and tell the men to put everything back in the house … that they'd changed their minds. But it was no use. They carried all her material things. And those material things carried her happy memories. She watched as the men waved goodbye to her children.

The group had become buddies for the day in the middle of so much chaos. *Probably for the best. At least the moving men were a happy inspiration for the kids.* However, all Julia could think was, *please don't go! Wake me up from this nightmare.*

Julia looked at her children, then at Tom who glanced around, before catching her eye. He gave his wife a half smile and breathed out a shaky, emotional sigh. Moving was hard on him, too. He may not have been as attached to life in Troy as his wife, but the mourning was no less real. Then he took his hand and put it on the back of their smallest son's shoulders, with a glance down to him and his other children, Tom smiled.

"We are moving on to bigger and better things," Tom said aloud, for his whole family to hear.

Julia held her breath; she wanted to feel the same, but she most definitely did not. *Not even a little.* She wanted to be glad about moving on, but just couldn't. Positive thinking didn't help. God knows she tried! She just couldn't shake the feeling of being forced to leave the one and only place she called home.

People kept telling her home was wherever her family was. Of course, they tried all kinds of words to make her feel better – to be okay with the move. But to Julia, she needed more than her husband and kids. Right or wrong, she did. Her community was a huge part of her life. And she was leaving all that behind.

They stood in front of the house just staring long after the moving van had pulled away. *This* was home. How could she ever feel okay being separated from it?

****

A few hours later, after the house was cleaned from

top to bottom for the new owners, they packed their last few things into Tom's black BMW parked in the small, hilled driveway. The light snow in front of the house glistened from the outdoor lights near the garage and you could see all the moving men's footprints in the snow.

Julia threw her purse carelessly into the front seat of the car and told the children to put on their seatbelts. In that instant she realized what was happening. *Wait, was this it? Could this really BE IT? We are leaving.*

As Julia stood in the driveway with the car door open, readying herself for the dreaded drive, she turned and looked longingly once more at the brick, tan, and green ranch home she loved so much.

Now you belong to someone else, she thought. *You're not mine anymore.* Her heart sank, as memories flashed through her mind. Memories of her children running around in the snow. Memories of summer when they'd run and jump on the slip and slide out back or when they'd run through the sprinkler on hot days while she served bright red Kool Aid.

She remembered the kids in the neighborhood riding their bikes in the kiddie parade – going down the street together during the Fourth of July gathering. It was the first year after they moved in. Sara and Kyle were so happy to be in the parade. As the kids rode by on new bikes she had just bought, Tom quickly took pictures as he yelled out to their children, "Way to go, Sara, and Kyle! Smile!" He said, as he chased after them, clicking away on his camera.

Julia remembered sitting under the stars with Tom as they sipped wine on summer nights after the children had gone to bed. She recalled Christmas mornings, when the children came running down the hallway to the family tree in the living room and ripped open their gifts with joy!

She remembered the first time her parents had seen their new home and how happy they were for them. She recalled sitting with her father at their small kitchen table eating breakfast. He commented to her how very happy she seemed to be in their new home. "It must be bringing you great joy!" he continued, as they enjoyed coffee and eggs. "I have never seen you this happy before. You are simply glowing!"

Then Julia shook her head and sharply cut off the flood of memories. She lifted her hand to her face and wept. The children sat silently in the car, staring out the window toward their mother as she cried. They, too, realized in that moment that this was it. They were about to leave their home and wouldn't be coming back. The children looked at each other, and then looked back out the window toward their mother. Thomas started to cry, and Kyle hung his head. Sara looked at the house with her mother in the foreground ... still crying.

"It's a sad day," Sara stated, in the back seat as Tom walked around the car to embrace his wife. "It's a sad day."

Sweet Sixteen

"Happy Birthday to You! Happy Birthday to You! Happy Birthday dear Becca, Happy Birthday to YOU!" sing my friends. Its 1996 and my mother and Zander are snuggled up together and singing along in the kitchen.

"AND MANY MORE!" my mother manages to ring out afterward, completely out of tune, as usual. "Phew! I got it in there. If you don't say it, you're cursed!"

All my friends from school look at me weird. "It's a family thing," I mutter, as I fidget because everyone is now staring at me. I really don't like being the center of attention.

My old friend, Stacey, chimes in, "Okay, aren't you going to blow out your candles?"

"Yes!" This year's cake is my favorite: chocolate cake with chocolate icing and a yellow border with bright pink, flaming candles. I lean toward the flickering flames and blow.

Whhhhhhhh. I wasn't sure I'd have enough breath for all sixteen candles, but I did. Failing to blow them all out would probably curse me, too. And I definitely don't need any more problems!

"Did you make a wish?" asks Stacey.

"Yes, but I can't say what it is, or it won't come true." I feel my face turn red as I recall the wish.

"I know what it is, or should I say *who* it is?" Emily

says, as she gives me a familiar look.

"I know, I know," I say to her. Then all my friends glance over at Emily. It just takes a quick glance at her face to give away what she's talking about.

"Oh, geez, not him again! No more boy talk, people! It's a slumber party. Let's forget about dumb boys for one night and have some fun!" Stacey insists.

"I second that," says my mother, as she leans across the table to cut the small store-bought cake, that simply says "Happy Birthday" on it. She dishes it out onto small pink paper plates and gives us all forks and napkins.

"Here you go, girls!" she says, as everyone pounces on their cake.

It's 8 p.m. on Friday and my mother has invited my friends over, to a slumber party for my sixteenth birthday. We just finished watching an early *Phantom of the Opera* in black and white. The movie was silent and the guy playing the phantom looked like he should have been cast as some sort of living dead character instead.

It's a freaky start to the night, and I got some odd looks from my friends. My mom also rented the *Twilight Zone*, trying to make it a Halloween-spooky themed party. But my friends aren't buying it and have decided to try to scare each other for entertainment instead.

"This is boring," says Emily. "I know, I'm bored, too!" states Stacey.

I'm pretty sure no teenager sits still long enough to even watch a movie when their friends are near. My mother puts in the second tape and as soon as they see it's black and white, they're bored all over again. *Great, now everyone's going to think I'm some weirdo. Way to go, Mom!*

I take my piece of cake and pop a bit into my mouth.

Then I set my plate down on the table so I can get to the presents, ignoring the film. I pick up the first one, when my mother suggests we gather up the gifts and take them to the coffee table in our family room.

"It's more comfortable in there," she insists. *We weren't uncomfortable, but okay.* We make her happy and move to the couch, sitting our stuff down on the coffee table. Everyone soon piles their gifts on top of each other, on the small table in a heap in front of where I am sitting.

"Open your gifts, Becca!" says Stacey, with a smile and her eyes wide-open beaming at me. "I can't wait for you to see what I got you!"

As I lift up the beautifully wrapped box I've been eyeing, I read the card aloud first, and then tear into it. Inside is a gorgeous medium size water globe, with a small frog reading a book on a lifted toadstool. When you shake it, glitter falls all around the figure. "You know me so well!" I say to Stacey after seeing the nice gift. "I'll definitely have to put this on my desk. I can use it as a paperweight!" I say with delight and Stacey smiles back at me with joy.

I love frogs AND reading. All my friends know it. I usually read a book a week. It started as a fun competition between Emily and me, trying to see who could read the most books in a week. But then the more and more I read, the further determined I was to keep reading just to see how many books I could get through. It became my own personal challenge. And now it seems like second nature to read something every day. So, this is the perfect gift for me!

"Wow!" everyone says, as I hold it up to show them, shaking it some more so the glitter keeps rolling around inside. It makes a glitter rainbow, falling all around the content little frog, as he reads his book.

"Thanks, Stacey," I say again, looking over at her nervously still hating all the attention, even though it's positive. She was just about to bite into her piece of cake, but she still manages to smile at me anyway.

"You're welcome." Her voice is all muffled, stuffed full of cake. But she continues anyway, "I know you love frogs and books."

"I do! I love it." I place the snow globe back in its box for protection and move on to the next gift.

"This one is from Lilly," I inform my friends, as I show off the pink and green wrapped squishy package.

Lilly anxiously grabs one of the couch pillows and clutches it to her chest, rocking back and forth with excitement while she waits for me to open it.

"More frogs!" I announce happily, as I unwrap it to see a green frog t-shirt. It unfolds as I pick it up, so I go ahead and get a hold of the shoulders for better viewing and turn it around for everyone to see. As I do that, a pair of socks falls from the bundle.

"Oh, and matching frog socks! Cool!"

"See? Your frog obsession is no secret!" Lilly giggles. Her adorable round face leans in for another bite of cake, but she misses. As the cake falls to the plush carpet, we all stop and look at each other. I begin to laugh. It's infectious and soon we're all giggling!

The next gift is in a cute black gift bag, with fake diamonds forming a center circle and the words, "BIRTHDAY GIRL" written in glitter; white speckled tissue paper peeking out the top.

"That's from me!" Lexi shouts proudly.

I reach in and pull out a white box with green ribbon on it, that has a little window in the top, giving me a glimpse of the contents. "Chocolates!!"

We all squeal, and I immediately rip off the ribbon and dig in. Although I want to eat them all myself (*who wouldn't!*), I pass the box so my friends can each have a piece.

"Just one!" I beg. But I know they won't eat them all.

Allison hands me a card. "I didn't know what to get you this year."

I open the pink envelope and see the money inside. Allison wrote some really sweet things about me and said I should "buy something that makes you smile." Then she signed it, "Friends forever."

"Now mine," Emily says shyly, as she hands me a flat rectangular package with purple and white paper and a shiny purple, girly bow stuck in the middle.

First, I shake it.

"Why on earth would you shake it? Just open it!" Lexi cries.

"My brother likes Legos, so I thought I'd see what it was like to have a present that made noise!"

We all laugh and sigh, a little impatient waiting on the last treat to be revealed.

I carefully remove the bow. We reuse those kinds of things all the time. Then I flip the package over and run my finger through the paper seam to remove the paper. There's tissue paper under the wrapping paper, protecting what's inside.

When I eventually get all the paper off, I flip it back over. It's a framed picture of Emily and me from last summer at the pool. We're in our swimsuits, sharing a lounge chair, beach towels thrown around our shoulders, sun-kissed skin, and our hair wet, hanging straight down our faces. Laughing at who knows what, but I remember that day. We were happy. Carefree.

Now I feel like crying, my emotions getting away

from me because of the simple, thoughtful gift. But I hold back the tears. Instead, I make a funny comment about the picture and turn it around for everyone to see.

"We were laughing at the guys who think they're 'all that' at the pool! Strutting around like God's gift. But we all known the lifeguards are the only hot ones!"

Everyone laughs and nods in agreement and my happy tears are back under control.

As the gift-opening comes to an end, my friends throw out suggestions for new entertainment.

"Cards!"

"Charades!"

"Truth or dare!"

"Hide-and-seek in the dark!"

"I don't care what we do, but keep the snacks coming!"

Everyone gets up to set their plates on the counter in the kitchen and get something to drink. Then we retreat to my bedroom for a game. Next order of business ... Truth or Dare!

"This is gonna be fun!" agree my friends, as we leave the kitchen and head down the hall toward my bedroom.

"Come on, Becca!" Allison calls to me. "I already have a good one!" she claims, as she jumps through my doorway into my bedroom.

"Fine, I'll be right there. I need to go to the bathroom."

"Okay, but hurry!" my friends yell back, then slam my bedroom door.

While I'm in the bathroom, I decide I might as well wash my face, because tonight clearly isn't going to be a normal face-routine kind of night. And I *have* to wash my face every morning and every night, unless I want another breakout. I pick up my foaming face wash and turn on the hot water.

Squirting out the orange, gooey cleanser into my hand, I lather it up, and spread it over my face, moving in circular motions. When my whole face is covered and I've rubbed my skin to my own satisfaction, I gather the warm water in my hands and splash it up to my face to rinse. Usually, I get water all over the countertop in this process, but I always wipe it dry with the hand towel afterwards.

As I towel-dry my face, I notice something odd. It's quiet. There are several girls at my house, in my bedroom, and it's quiet. Girls aren't quiet. My bedroom and the bathroom share a wall and it's *definitely* too quiet. *That's strange. I should hear them.*

I hang my towel on the rod next to the sink, then I stand still to listen.

Nothing.

Not a single sound is coming from my room, from anywhere for that matter. A house full of teenage girls, no sound? Girls who are supposed to be playing a game of truth or dare, aren't quiet.

I step into the hallway, dark as always, when I hear my mother's voice.

"Becca, is that you, hon?"

"Yes, Mom," I respond, as I walk toward her to see what she wants or needs me to do. Cause I'm sure that's it. She probably wants me to clean up or something, while she's getting Zander ready for bed. *I see it coming.*

As I approach her, I see she's hugging Zander close to her side. He's getting so big. *Try holding him, the dog, a knife, and looking for ghosts. Well that was when he was two, of course I wouldn't hold him now.*

"Can you clean up your friends' mess for me, before you guys start playing around? I don't want to have to do it in the morning. We still have church tomorrow after everyone leaves."

"Alright," I say to her, with a tinge of irritation in my voice, disappointed at having to clean and miss out on the first of the fun my friends were having.

"Thanks, sweetie," she replies, as she walks toward Zander's bedroom to help him.

I pick up the plates and forks from the counter and clean as quickly as I can. I pitch the paper plates in the trash under the sink and open the dishwasher. When the forks and cake knife are rinsed, I load them along with the miscellaneous dishes that have piled up by the sink. The dishwasher is full, so I fill the detergent compartment, shut the door, and hit the start button.

When I feel my duty is done, I dry my hands and hang the dish towel back on the dishwasher handle like always. *That didn't take too long.*

Feeling pretty good about myself for being so efficient and finally being able to join my friends once again, I head toward my bedroom. My mother has the hall lights off as usual. Normally it bothers me, but in my happiness, I don't think too much about the darkness this time, as I walk down the hall.

As I reach my bedroom, I hear sound. *That's more like it.* The first familiar voice I recognize is my friend, Lexi Hutchins. It sounds like she's repeating a sentence over and over. *Weird.* I stand on the other side of the door listening for a moment, to what she's saying and try to make sense of it, when I suddenly feel a cold draft come down the hall.

I look down my legs, then back down the hall to see if I can tell where the chill is coming from, but it's too dark. I can't see anything at my feet and the only thing I can make out is the thin, glowing light coming from beneath my door.

"Dang," I say under my breath from the cold air, still trying to find a reason behind the draft.

Even though it is only a few days into March, it was hot earlier in my bedroom with everyone crammed in it before we opened gifts. So, I shed the flannel I had on and changed into my summer nightgown. Now I'm regretting that decision. Looking down at my legs with chills coursing throughout my body I can tell that all the hair on my body now stands on end.

That's so strange!

Suddenly, I hear the backdoor slam.

BANG!

And I nearly jump out of my skin. *What the heck is going on?*

I have a bad feeling. Too many weird things are happening. This is not a good sign. *Come on house, not during my sweet sixteen party! Don't I deserve at least one night of happiness?* Fight or flight kicks in, as my fear overtakes me.

I turn the doorknob to my bedroom to get to the safety of a group, but when I try to open the door, it won't move. I twist the knob again, harder this time, and push, but it still won't budge. It feels like somebody is on the other side holding it shut.

Now I'm just annoyed that I can't get into my own bedroom, so I try again, this time pushing against the door with my shoulder, throwing my body weight into it.

"You guys!" I cry out, "What are you doing? Let me in!"

It felt like I had been pushing against the door

forever, thinking it'll give way at any moment. But suddenly, without warning, the opposing force from the other side stops and my bedroom door swings wide open, hitting the back wall. I, of course, go flying in, no warning or time to protect myself, falling face first into my shag green carpet from the 1970s.

Shaking my head, confused as ever, I slowly pull myself up on my knees, a little dazed. I thought I'd find my friends standing over me with their arms out, offering to help me up. It had to seem weird on their side, hearing me yell out that the door was stuck, banging on the door, pushing against the door, watching me fall into the room as the door slammed open. I figured they were at least laughing at my expense.

But I'm wrong! Looking up from the atrocious green carpet, I can't believe my eyes. There sat my friends in their nightgowns on the floor at the foot of my bed in front of my window in a circle. In the center of the circle, I see my mother's candle from the dining room. It's a few inches tall with a brass shiny holder and it's lit. I remember my grandmother gave it my mother for an anniversary present for my parents when they were together.

"What in the hell?" I mumble, as I look around and pull myself to my feet in disbelief. No one seems to even notice I dropped in. *Literally!*

Everyone's eyes are closed, and Lexi appears to be leading the group. She's sitting in the middle facing the window with her back toward me chanting, "Come, come, come, …"

"Come?" I question aloud. "What is going on?" I insist, but no one responds. I'm not even sure they hear me. Their eyes remain closed.

Finally, on my feet, I move behind Lexi who is still

chanting, as if trying to summon the devil, "Come, come, come, ..."

The Catholic girl in me is terrified. *Why is she doing this? WHAT is she doing? Why can't anyone hear me?*

"Come into our circle," Lexi chants again. "Come to us. We want to see you," she goes on. Then without warning, her eyes fly open and she roars, "SHOW YOURSELF NOW!!"

I'm beyond freaked out and shriek in surprise. It might seem harmless if you didn't grow up Catholic and if you didn't have a house that weirded you out most of your life, but this isn't right.

"NOOO!" I scream at the top of my lungs. But I'm too late.

A NEW LIFE

Julia picked up the box cutter they were using to open the cardboard boxes, and picked up a box, placing it in front of herself. Then she took the cutter in her hand again and carefully lifted it up to her eyes to view it more closely. She placed it at the left side of the box, held the box still, and carefully sliced toward the right in a straight line, until she reached the end. The box popped opened.

What's in this box? Julia put down the box cutter without another glance. She put her hands inside the cardboard and began pulling out its contents, revealing books from the shelves that used to be in their family room.

Suddenly, an image of their two free standing bookshelves packed full of her book collection from their house in Troy entered her thoughts. With a book from her collection in her hand, the pain from the move triggered her emotions and she started to cry. Bringing the book close to her heart, she let the pain that welled up inside her body flood out. She cried so hard she gasped for air barely getting any. And she didn't care.

Falling to her knees onto the ceramic floor, she was thankful to be alone right now. Tom and the kids left to shop for groceries and other basic home decor items for the new house, leaving her to unpack.

Julia cried and cried, allowing the pain that she had been hiding for days to finally consume her. As she did, more images of the home she missed so much came to her mind. It had only been four days, but it already felt like a lifetime to Julia.

Her memories came flooding back as she let her mind walk through her old family room. She stood in front of their light-colored wooden entertainment center with their wedding pictures on top, as well as pictures of the kids from babies to present school pictures, all framed and laid out elegantly. Then they had a large print of a family picture; Julia had made them drive to Elder-Beerman in Dayton to get. She remembered getting herself all done up for the picture and then dressing up each child as they tried to fight her off. "I don't want a picture," Kyle cried, as Julia tried to secure a bow tie around his neck. "I don't like you or cameras."

The wooden wall unit contained their television and Julia's new CD player that Tom had gotten her for her birthday. *It was so expensive*! She could remember him boasting about the CD player for weeks! He wouldn't stop talking about how he had taken so much time with the store clerk to look at several players and go over each one's special features, to be sure to select the best one for her. You could tell he felt so manly as he spoke to her about the CD player's features as if it were the most precious machine in the world. Julia hardly paid attention. She was taken aback over the expensive gift and his kind gesture.

She could see the brick fireplace as she turned to the right, and the little brick cut-out window into the kitchen. She remembered the black glazed mini bar countertop beneath the small brick opening and Tom's happily displayed Brandy and Port bottles.

Her children used to love the brick window. She reminisced about how they'd play peek-a-boo with Mommy through the small opening when they were really young. As she would dry dishes, be cooking, or if she were simply just getting them juice from the fridge. She would laugh as they would giggle and say, "Silly Mommy," as Julia made goofy, silly faces through the opening.

Then she remembered her family's sitting area in front of the wooden entertainment center so they could see the television set. Their two floral printed couches with pink pillows, and their small wooden coffee table placed perfectly in front of them. *It held so many drinks, snacks, and gifts over the years.* Sara was the child who really loved to do homework on the coffee table trying to sneak some TV time between homework lessons. It took her forever to get her lessons done. Julia remembered endless fights with Sara, trying to get her to turn off the TV or do her homework at the dinner table.

"It would be so much easier if you would just move to the dinner table to finish your assignments," Julia would say.

"No, Mom!" She would fight back, "I'm fine. I'll get it done." Then she would take another forty-five minutes until she completed her assignment.

As Julia recalled the past in their old home, she felt her heart sink even deeper into her chest. She remembered how she couldn't stop herself from crying the week before the move and found herself right back there now. She had been trying so hard to stop herself from going down that road again, but she clearly had no control over her emotions. So, she just let herself feel all the pain and loss. Embraced it. Owned it. She thought it was the only way she might heal.

****

Tom smiled as he walked around the grocery store with his children while they shopped.

"Now, did you ask if you could have that?" he asked Thomas, as he caught the boy sneaking fruit snacks into the grocery cart.

"No, Daddy," replied Thomas, with embarrassment as he hung his head.

"Just ask me next time first and maybe you can have them."

"Okay," Thomas said sadly to his father, with his head toward the floor.

"Daddy?"

"What?"

"Can I please have fruit snacks?" asked Thomas, with his bottom lip appropriately sticking out as he looked up at his dad.

"Okay, you may," he answered as his son jumped up into his arms, barely giving Tom time to let go of the grocery cart to catch him.

Tom smiled and scooped up his small son in an embrace and gave him a big hug and kiss. "You know how cute you are, don't you?"

"Yes," Thomas answered, shyly but honestly. Tom placed him back down on the floor. Thomas' blond hair and blue eyes lit up with excitement, as he jumped up on the side of the cart, to drop the fruit snack box into the shopping cart.

"God love him!" said Tom, as he looked at his other two children watching all the action and smiling silently at their cute little brother.

Yes, things were finally going well again. His wife seemed to be getting back to normal. As normal as things could be after moving into a new house and to a new town where she didn't want to be.

The town wasn't truly new for his wife. Julia had grown up here and her parents still lived nearby. Tom hoped they would help take a load off of Julia and hopefully help ease her depression. Maybe they could even go on a vacation! *God, that'd be nice,* thought Tom. *We haven't had a vacation alone in years!*

Tom smiled at the possibility of getting back to a happy norm.

Yes, as soon as school starts, I imagine things will be back to normal again.

Or at least that's what he hoped.

****

Julia turned off the shower and pulled back the plain pink curtain. It was 6 a.m. on a blustery cold January day in Ohio. She was already awake because she couldn't sleep, so she decided to get up and get ready before the kids woke up. It was day six in their new home and Julia was trying to perk up and be less angry about the move. More positive for her family. Less selfish. She was trying to replace her negative thoughts with happier visions, but every time she started unpacking, she'd find something that triggered a memory of her happier days in their old home. *There are no rightful places for our belongings here.* As much as she tried, she just didn't feel right placing their things around the house. *It's just not the same.* And the tears would roll again. Knowing she had to stay positive for her children, and actually being positive for her children were two different things. It would be so much easier to roll up in a ball and let her pain consume her.

She tried to unpack when no one was around to at least spare them the awkward spectacle she made of herself. It was predictable by now: she would barely open a box, pick out one item, and start crying. She didn't want to keep coming unhinged in front of her family.

Meanwhile, Julia already had problems beyond her own negative feelings from the move. Her son, Kyle, had been acting out again by leaving the house without permission and not telling her where he was going. The kids had just started at their new schools and already he was having issues.

The last few days she had turned around to find him missing when he had just been sitting behind her at the kitchen table eating dinner. He was just gone. Quietly sneaking away.

When she asked Sara where Kyle had gone or if he had said anything before leaving, all Sara did was shrug her shoulders and say, "I don't know. He just walked out the side door. He didn't say anything to me."

Julia put down the dishes and buried her head in her hands. Then she reached for a hand towel to dry off and walked to the back door to look out. And, as had become the new normal, she couldn't see a trace of her son.

Where'd he go? She knew she had to be on top of it even though she hadn't felt on top of anything since long before the move. Unfortunately, she no longer had the energy.

SÉANCE

The wind rapidly whips through my bedroom. Soon my curtains are flying and flailing about, as if a tornado is hitting only my room. Everything on my dresser flies off hitting the shag carpet: hair clips, picture frames, money, necklaces – everything. Over the chaos I hear Lexi continue her chant leading my other friends to join her: "Come, come, come, ..." ignoring what is happening around them.

"WHO? Who on earth do you think is coming?!" I yell but get no response.

My mother's white candle from our dinner table (*that Lexi took without permission*) blows around furiously struggling to stay lit.

Suddenly, a deep male voice moans from within the circle, as my friends continue their chant. It's a low, dark moan that noticeably is in sync with the room's windy tornado. It doesn't sound happy!

The room's environment and presence completely change, and we all feel evil enter the room. The freak wind continues and the trinkets that were on top of my desk fall so hard to the floor that they break on the carpet! *How could something fall that hard that it would break on shag carpet?*

"Come, come, come, ..." Lexi repeats the chant, uncaring and seemingly oblivious of the turmoil around her. Her eyes are still closed, and the other girls just sit around her on the floor in a circle as if stuck in place. Some of the girl's eyes are closed and some wide open watching the events take place around them without moving.

She's allowing evil into my room and my house. Actually, she's inviting it in! I don't get this! Why? Why would someone want to do this?

What my friends probably started as good, fun entertainment quickly turns into something very real and very sinister.

I can't stand it any longer.

"WHAT THE HELL IS GOING ON?" I scream as loud as I can, while I run toward Lexi. Hopefully, I'm heard this time! I'm fed up and I'm not waiting for a reply anymore. Swiftly, without thinking, I jump on Lexi's back to stop her.

I misjudge the space between Lexi and Stacey and hit the floor hard in the middle of the circle, falling on my stomach. As I look up at my friends, I see that no one has moved, and no one appears fazed by my fall into the circle. *Come on... How could THAT not get a reaction from you all?* They sit motionless with their legs crossed in front of them, maintaining their circle.

I ignore their lack of reaction and look for my next best plan to stop this nonsense: my mother's candle. I immediately reach over into the circle for it, bring it to my lips and blow. *Puff!* The flame goes out and my friends open their eyes and scream.

I scramble to my feet as fast as I can and go for the light switch. The last thing I need is for my mother to come in here and find this.

The light comes on and I can finally see my friends' faces, all of them twisted in terror, mouths gaped open. All but one friend – Lexi. She's standing with one hip cocked tapping her foot clearly irritated. *She's irritated? I'm mortified!* Her arms are crossed and there's a big scowl on her face. Her eyebrows standing upright with anger, breathing in heavily, nostrils flaring out. Obviously ready to fight for whatever reason. I have seen her mad before, but this is unreal.

"Becca! Just what do you think you are doing? You just ruined everything!"

"Are you kidding me?" I exclaim loudly, as our friends stand by and watch the show.

"Excuse me?"

"Yeah," I say to her as the familiar fear and adrenaline bubble up from the pit of my stomach rising toward my heart and ready for the fight.

"I don't know what the hell is going on in here, but this ... this is MY ROOM. MY HOUSE! And you don't have permission to do what you're doing! You don't have the RIGHT!! You can't play around with summoning the devil and crap. That isn't funny, Lexi.

"What if what you chanted to was a real thing? What if it worked and something just came into my house that's evil? And during my birthday party! How could you?" I rant at her, shaking my finger as I walk closer.

Nearly hyperventilating and shaking from anger, I walk right up to her. She needs to be confronted. I had to keep my courage up and keep going!

We stand toe-to-toe in the middle of the now broken circle with the dinner table candle lying on its side at our feet.

"Just what did you think you were doing?" my voice exposing just how mad I am with her.

"Oh, come on, Becca!" she argues back at me. "You really don't think this looked fun?"

"Fun?" I yell. "NO!" *For sure my eyes popping out of my head.* ...

"You are such a ninny," Lexi insists, speaking to me like I'm beneath her. She's just standing there, her arms still crossed, still in "angry Lexi" mode. Then she raises her hand toward her face, to bite at a nonexistent hangnail, to look as though she doesn't care a thing about what I'm saying.

"What?" I say as I throw my hands up in the air, then land them on my hips.

"Yeah, you are so boring," she continues, as she turns toward the others as they watch this ordeal unfold. "I told ya she'd be like this. Boring Becca!" Lexi turns back my way. "I knew you wouldn't want to do anything cool tonight, so I waited until you left."

Then she turns back to the others. "You all had fun, right?" she asks our friends, but they just look at her dumbfounded.

"Lexi?" I call, as she tries to get the others to respond in her defense. Hearing my voice, she slowly turns back to me with annoyance and continues biting her nail in frustration.

"Yes?"

"Who *exactly* were you asking to come?" My fists stay clenched at my sides, but I hope she doesn't notice. It would just lead to more harassment.

Man, do I want to hit her right in the face and hit her hard! She's always pulling stunts. Well, I'm done this time. Done! I vow right here and now that this is the last time I'll ever hang out with her.

"I was summoning my father," she replies.

"What?" I say back to her. "Wait a minute. Your father?"

"Yes! My father!" she shouts, this time up in my face

and with double the attitude.

"I don't understand," I say, as everyone watches. By now all my girlfriends have their hands over their mouths, shocked at the scene playing out before them.

"What don't you understand? My father is DEAD!!"

Lexi breaks our gaze and walks toward the corner of my bedroom while we all watch not knowing what to do with this news. However, we all know she tends to be a bit melodramatic. This is most likely a big fat lie! *A ploy for attention,* is what I immediately think.

Typical Lexi. She'll do anything for attention and mostly negative attention at that. Her father is probably alive and well and she is just making this whole thing up for a pity party.

Putting my hand up to our friends so they give me a minute and just wait until I'm finished, I take two seconds to think before I speak again. "I'm over this! Your little game didn't work! Your jokes are not funny at all! ENOUGH!!"

Taking in a deep breath I know I need to deal with this situation gingerly. Calming myself down, I muster up more courage from deep down inside. Slowly, I make my way toward her and put my hand on her shoulder, but Lexi quickly brushes it off and walks away from me.

"Lexi, I'm sorry," I say to her. *Gross, I hate saying those words to her. It's not even true, but I have to keep the peace and get an answer from her.*

I try to sound more caring, but I just can't keep all the frustration out of my voice and it shows. And how she responds will help us know if this is true or just one of her terrible jokes. She has a history of stirring up trouble and lying; it's hard not to second-guess everything that comes out of her mouth.

Lexi is one of those friends that you have, because when she's nice, she's nice. We have so much fun! But then she can be super mean; and you hate her. Really hate her. *And that's more often, than any of us care to admit.* In our friend group, we're almost afraid to get rid of her. So, we don't exclude her from anything for fear of retaliation. She's one of those "keep your enemies close" kind of people. Sad, but true. I guess you could truly say we were frenemies!

"How did you father die?"

"He killed himself," responds Lexi nonchalantly, still obviously irritated, and very much avoiding looking at me. She seems to find my raspberry pink bedroom walls super interesting instead and is looking right at them, as if amused. But whether she's truly irritated, sad, or confused, I'm not sure.

But I'll err on the side of kindness.

"Oh my, God." You could hear everyone suck in a collective breath, at the news.

"Lexi!" I cry and make my way back over to her. Although her back is still facing me as she bites her nail and contemplates my bedroom walls, I can't *not* go to her. That's what you do when people are hurting. And fighting friends are no exception. I'm a good person; it's what you do.

"I'm so sorry. We had no idea." She finally faces me when she hears my voice so close behind her.

"It's no big deal, I guess."

"No big deal? It's definitely a big deal. It's a big deal to us. You wanna talk about it?" I reach for her hand to comfort her and for once she lets me. Our friends watch in shock, their hands still covering their mouths as they fight back emotions, all while wondering if Lexi is telling the truth.

"Not really. Not now anyway, but thanks. He died when I was a baby so I never knew him. My Mom and I don't ever talk about it and I don't ask."

"Wow. Lexi, I just ..." I trail off, looking down at my feet, as I think and take this all in. "That's so sad, Lexi. Can I ask, where'd it happen?"

"In prison."

KYLE STRIKES AGAIN

Julia woke up to the phone ringing. *What now?* She thought as she sat up, groggy and fumbling for the switch to turn on a nearby lamp on the nightstand. All she wanted was a little rest and some alone time. But that wasn't going to happen this morning, apparently.

Sitting up in bed, she picked up the ringing phone from her nightstand.

"Hello," she groaned.

"Hello, is this Mrs. Walter?" asked a male voice on the end of the line.

"Yes," she replied, hoping it wasn't another dang telemarketer who had just interrupted her sleep!

"This is Mr. Seekins, principal of Middleton Middle School."

Oh no! She tried to hold the phone steady in her hand after hearing who the caller was, knowing it could only be a bad call regarding Kyle.

"Mrs. Walter, I'm afraid that I am calling about Kyle. He pulled the fire alarm today at school and I need you or his father to come in to discuss it with me and take him home."

"Oh no," replied Julia, without being able to stop the words from coming out. "I'm very sorry, sir! I will be right in," Julia assured the principal.

He proceeded to tell her a few of the details over the phone, but she'd already stopped listening. She thankfully caught his *goodbye*. "Goodbye, see you in a few minutes." And with that, she hung up the tangle-corded receiver and hopped out of bed to get dressed.

About 10 minutes later, Julia pulled up to her son's new school prepared for the worst. She had been through this before with Kyle at his old school. It was apparent that he was looking for some sort of attention, but she just didn't understand why. But pulling fire alarms? She had thought of a few things to discuss with the school staff on her way. Of course, they needed to get Kyle some sort of help, but Julia didn't know where to start. She and Tom tried before but couldn't find someone they thought would be a good fit. And now they were at their wits' end.

****

After two hours in the principal's office, Julia and Kyle went home. Julia walked into the kitchen, placed her heavy suede bag on the countertop and took off her winter coat. It was early in the afternoon so the other two kids weren't home from school yet. Kyle's school had suggested taking Kyle home early for a lesson. As Julia turned to chat with Kyle, she saw he was already in the hallway near his room. Julia heard the door slam shut and that was that. She certainly was at her limit and out of ideas.

Julia picked up the phone to call her husband and beg him to come home and help her. *I can't do this anymore.* She could no longer deal with Kyle alone. Starting now.

But as soon as she started to dial, she realized she didn't have Tom's new work number. He hadn't given it to her yet. It was only his third day at his new job. Julia's guilt kicked in. *I can't bug him already.* It was important, but there was nothing he could do to help her solve this problem right now, so she set down the receiver.

Julia was well aware that finding a professional in Akron to help Kyle was a necessity but had no idea where to start. She'd thought the school would have some recommendations, but they just gave her a list of options, unable to recommend someone specific who may be a good fit for their family. Kyle also refused to speak to the school's guidance counselor, so that didn't help. The principal told Julia when Kyle was in the counselor's office all he did was slowly slouch down in his chair until he fell asleep.

How on earth will I get him to go if he wouldn't even listen to the school's guidance counselor?

Julia was sitting at the counter, hunched over, preoccupied by her pounding head, when Kyle walked back into the room.

She rubbed her temples harder trying to think of her next move and wipe away a little stress at the same time.

"I'm going to the bookstore!" announced Kyle casually, as if he weren't just suspended from school. Kyle didn't wait for a response; he just continued walking past the kitchen where his mother sat and vanished through the side door without another word. He was gone.

Julia turned. From her small view point she could glimpse him walking through the snow-covered gate in their backyard as the snow slowly came down. Soon he was out of sight.

That's it. I'm done.

****

Kyle walked to the bookstore. The clerk from the main desk area shouted out a random welcome greet without even looking up from his magazine as Kyle stepped into the store. He didn't even notice that Kyle was a teenager.

Kyle strolled to the back of the store where the magazines were sold and looked around to see if anyone else was there. He picked up a magazine and looked intently at the pictures. The women in the photos were gorgeous and he wondered if he would ever get to see a woman like that in person one day.

Their tan slender bodies were so perfect, with flawless makeup on their beautiful faces. He was so lost in thought looking at the magazine that he didn't notice someone coming toward him. He heard someone cough and snapped back to reality, looking up from his adult material.

"Oh, hey Henry," Kyle said, as he closed the magazine and placed it back on the shelf just as he had found it. Then he turned to chat with his buddy.

"What's up?" Henry was just an average teenager trying to find his place in the world: pale blue eyes, dyed jet-black hair, spiked mohawk … nose ring, and he was obviously skipping school. Kyle had seen him a few times in passing and had hung out with him and his buddies briefly after school since moving into the neighborhood.

"Not much. What are you doing in here today?"

A grin formed on Henry's face, "Um, I think I could ask you the same question. Aren't you supposed to be in school or something?"

Kyle stopped for a second to think of what to say next. "Yeah, but …" Kyle trailed off shyly. His cheeks had the decency to turn a shade of pink as he recalled the reason for his absence. He didn't want to look un-cool in front of Henry and his buddies.

"I kinda pulled the fire alarm at school and got suspended."

"You what!" Henry smiled and giggled as he walked closer to Kyle. He proceeded to put his hand atop of Kyle's shoulder.

Kyle just shrugged his shoulders at this morning's disaster as if it meant nothing and was no big deal. "That kinda of thing happens every day, right!" Kyle told his newfound friend, his face getting even hotter.

"Whoa!" Henry exclaimed in surprise, his smirk getting even bigger.

Henry's buddies were nearby in a small, separate sitting area surrounded by bookshelves full of comics and graphic novels. Right where they wanted to be. Of course, the boys' current comic of choice happened to feature graphic pictures of barely dressed women cozied up to superheroes with shields and armor barely covering their revealing body parts.

Henry called over to his friends as they looked at their comics. "Hey guys, you have to hear this! You won't believe what Kyle did today!" He could barely contain his grinning face and excitement and let out a laugh, slapping Kyle on the back, as if rewarding Kyle's bad decision and behavior. "Listen to this!" he went on. "Kyle, tell them what you did at school today!"

SOMETHING'S WRONG IN THE HOUSE

I wake the next morning and just know that nothing will ever be the same.

Lexi leaves, thank God, and the others are packing up to go after my mom cooks us bacon and eggs for breakfast.

As we wait and pack up, no one speaks about what had happened last night. I think everyone's still upset about Lexi's chant and confused by her newest revelation. We don't argue often as friends so I'm sure there'll be plenty of talk about last night once we actually find words.

It's the news about her father that seems to be weighing on us the most. No one knew. And no one knew if she was even telling the truth because she's a compulsive liar. Her statement last night though, that was icing on the cake. *I had made up my mind and wouldn't be changing it. I was done with her.*

After the last person leaves, I head down the drafty hallway toward my bedroom once again. However, I don't make it very far, when a strange bolt of unease and adrenaline bursts through my body. The adrenaline starts at my feet and flows up toward my heart, and I know, I just know... something's wrong!

Swiftly the cold sensation changes and feels like a red-hot firecracker that morphs into a hard gum like substance, that gets stuck in the back of my throat. The red-hot feeling begins to feel like a cramp that makes its way throughout my body. Moving and snaking as it passes through my veins and then outward toward my arms and legs. The sensation is raw and leaves me feeling strange and jittery. Almost like I can't move or it will hurt me. *Maybe I'm having a heart attack? But I'm only 16! What's happening?!*

I feel like I should run from this place as fast as I can.

But when would I stop *running? Two blocks? When I hit a police station? The further away the better!*

Within the next couple minutes, the feeling starts to fade so I decide to walk back toward the family room for a bit. When I do, the hot sensation slows and eventually stops. *What is it about that dumb hallway?*

While looking down the hallway from the family room, I begin to piece things together. Most of the weird things seem to happen when I'm walking down this hallway. Finding comfort in my newfound safe space, I take in a deep breath for confidence. I want to test my theory so I step toward the hallway again.

Sure enough … the hot clay feeling begins to come back running under my skin and throughout my body. It continues as I step into the hallway and shows no sign of letting up or slowing down. In fact, it seems to burn even more this time.

"AHHH! What is that?" I blurt out, as I hear something coming from behind me now. *Is that my mom?* I stop and listen intently and don't hear it again, taking in my surroundings. Standing alone in the dimly lit hallway, everything looks as it should.

It seems like a *normal* day*! But nothing about this is normal!*

I turn back around and walk to my bedroom. I have

walked down this hall a million times since moving into this house nearly 6 years ago now, and never had I had a walk like that before! I don't feel alone.

An eerie feeling seems to follow me down the hallway watching every step I make until I reach my destination. I make a silent plea: *Please let me feel safe on the other side of my door! I can feel like something is about to happen the closer I get to my room.*

Taking the brass doorknob in my hand, I'm just as scared as I was the night of my birthday party. *My luck…* I twist it and push the door open and hope for the best. Stepping into my bedroom, which should be my safety-zone and sanctuary, I close the door behind me as fast as lightning!

"Whew!" I sigh with relief.

But then my brain catches up to my senses. That safe feeling I was hoping for. It's not here.

Leaning against my door for a moment, I stop to think. I want to go to my dresser and grab some clothes for the day. I haven't even gotten out of my PJ's for crying out loud when I hear an eerie sound. It sounds as if it's coming from the corner of my room where the girls had formed their circle the previous night. "Grrr …"

I freeze.

"Grrrr …" the grumbling sound comes again.

This time I *KNOW* I heard it. It's a deep, low growling sound.

Instantly, I feel as if I'm stuck in a horror movie! The kind my own mother won't let me watch!

I hesitantly grab clothes from the dark stained dresser, not even caring or looking at them, and make my way to my bathroom without looking back.

I dress in the bathroom, where I have one more

door between me and that creepy sound – so I feel a bit safer. The house does make settling noises, like my mother said in the past, but that certainly couldn't be one of them. Now I jump at every sound I hear.

****

Later that night we are wrapping up dinner and it's time to clean up the dishes after my mother's famously delicious, parmesan chicken in a white-wine olive oil sauce – my favorite!

"Bec, can you please clear the table while I get Zander ready for bed?" asks my mother, as she stands up and walks her dirty plate to the kitchen sink.

"Sure," I say, as I roll my eyes and remember that I just had my favorite meal so I should be nice and not complain or gripe like a normal teen.

"Come on, honey," says my mother, as she takes my little brother's hand and starts walking him out of the room toward the family room, on his way to bed. "Say goodnight to sissy!"

"Night, Zander!" I say, as I wave to him. He looks back at me, with a cute little smile and spark in his eye. "I'll see you tomorrow," still waving at him as he heads to bed, I can't help but notice his adorable little dimples and his pudgy little cheeks. *God, he's so adorable! And he knows it too!* I think to myself as I return to my task. That boy's cheeks are probably the only place on his whole body that the poor kid even has any fat! He's so skinny and hardly eats anything! The only thing he ever eats is Nutri-Grain Bars, pancakes, waffles, and yogurt, and that's every day.

I finish the last bit of dishes from our meal and stack them into our black and tan dishwasher, put in the dish-detergent, and close the door. I hit the wash button and hear the dishwasher start up. Hanging the dish rag over the dishwasher's handle to dry, I walk out of the kitchen and turn out the lights on my way. I'm feeling good. I almost want to whistle! It's been a good day and I completely forgot about all the strange occurrences from the night before and this morning.

Then I think of the growling sound and stop short near the fireplace. *I can't believe I forgot last night and this morning!* Replaying the sound in my mind, I can hear it like it just happened a moment ago and suddenly my happy mood is gone and is replaced with a low-terrifying, "Grrr…"

Just one more trek to my bedroom and I'm home free. *I'll be fine.* I tell myself, as I walk down the dark hallway, which seems to me like a scene from a haunted castle movie.

Tomorrow's a school day so I have to get some sleep. Mom will yell down the hall soon for me to go to bed, so I better get going. Gathering up some courage from deep down, I go into my bedroom and get my nightgown from my dresser drawer. Just like I had this morning, I take my clothes to the bathroom again and change. I can't help but feel a creepy unease in my room.

After I'm done getting ready in the bathroom, I call down the hall to my mother a quick, "night, Mom!" to which she replies in return, "night, hon." I push open my bedroom door and enter my dark room quickly switching on the light.

I am terrified to go to bed. I know I have to turn off the light so it's dark in my room. *If whatever it was, was growling at me in the daytime, what would it do in the DARK?!*

I know I have to just do it, turn off the light and

run to my bed. The only issues are: 1.) My bed and my light are really far apart from each other, I would have to run, and 2.) I am terrified.

Come on, Becca! I coach myself. *You have done this a hundred times. You can do this!*

Oh, I forgot! I have to set my alarm clock and pull out my clothes for school tomorrow. Geez, it never ends! I'll never make it through this haunted castle alive at this rate. I make it to the stained dresser that my mother inherited from her great-great grandmother. I take out a pair of underwear, jeans, and a t-shirt, then set them down on my desk chair near my bed. I'm about to go back to my light switch to turn it off and head to bed when…. I feel an abrupt cold air move the bottom of my nightgown.

That's odd. …

Soon the hair on my arms is standing on end. I've lived in this house for six years now and I've felt this kind of draft before. I can tell something isn't right.

I hastily turn off my light, then run to my bed, jump in it, and cover my head with my thick tan comforter. Now, my only protection between me and whatever it is in my room is the old comforter my sister has passed down to me.

For the next hour, I wait for something to happen and fall asleep.

****

Huh? I struggle to wake up after hearing something in my room. Opening my eyes wide, I hear some kind of movement. I try to grasp reality, I stay on my back afraid, unmoving, and facing the ceiling in terror.

Looking straight up, even though it's dark, I see a

strange white mist forming right over my head! As I look more intently at it, I see the mist shift and reshape itself into odd patterns until it forms into an apparition of a small child or baby. I can see it's dressed in a white flowing misty gown that wisps in the air as it hovers above me. It looks like it has eyes and possibly a baby bonnet on its head, like in the old days. It's very angelic and graceful. Its gown hovers outward into the night air as it moves gracefully without a sound.

At first, I am not afraid. I just stare and watch the oddity with wonder. Questions run rampant throughout my mind. But soon the misty shape opens its mouth into a perfect small circle. Then the graceful angelic child-like face turns into a horrific site.

I watch quietly as its eyes grow intent with evil, as they twist upwards into two piercingly sharp triangles. They shift into something you would see carved into a Halloween jack-o-lantern and I am reminded of a horror movie with Chucky or Freddy Krueger. The sides of its long, white, beautiful, flowing, mist-like gown form two arms that rapidly reach out toward me, as if to grab me.

Its mouth suddenly closes, and the entity's mist-like body shifts slightly to the right, then quickly whips back around toward me as if it's a pitcher on the mound at a baseball game about to throw. Then I see it! *What is that?*

Something big and black is in its hand! Only I can't see what it is. Its eyes flash like white lighting as they narrow in on me, then the white mist rapidly pitches the black object at me with detest. And everything goes black.

MIGRAINE AND MISERY

Tom came home from work and found Julia asleep on the couch. She couldn't get rid of her migraine, so she lay down while waiting for Kyle to come back. She must have drifted off to sleep.

Julia was overwhelmed and beside herself. She felt heaviness inside her heart that she just could not shake.

Why is the world so hard and why does it seem to be getting harder? Everyday there's a new problem.

She loved Tom, but why did she have to do it all herself? Everything fell on her at home. Simple stuff like clothes. Julia bought the kids clothes all year long. Tom never picked out anything for them, not even once!

She planned all the events in their lives, kept up with their school functions, and helped with homework. Every week, every month, year after year.

And then there were the extras that came with being a parent, such as scouts, soccer, baseball, and more! *She couldn't take it anymore!*

And why should she? Why should she have to find out what's wrong with Kyle on her own? Can't Tom help her do anything? Why is it always her against the world, solving every little problem herself? And don't forget the loads upon loads of laundry and cleaning the house and washing the dishes!

Why does she have to find a psychiatrist for Kyle?

Why can't Tom? She knew he would never offer. He wouldn't ever do that. The most he has ever done is talk to the kid and that went nowhere. *Hell, I can do that too!* She knew he wouldn't look into finding help in a million years! If she wouldn't do it, it just wouldn't get done!

Like everything else!

All he did was the yard work on the weekends. He didn't care for the children or put them to bed. He never made dinner, except that one time when she was having her nervous breakdown packing at the old house. That was months ago! No, no … if Julia didn't do it, it didn't get done!

Making dinner once in years, come on! Why couldn't he just step up a little and give her help? *Couldn't he see she needed it? Certainly, he could see that, couldn't he?* Julia just wanted help. *Why couldn't anyone just see it and step in to help her. Why?*

Soon she drifted off into sleep on the couch.

"Julia?" came Tom's voice. "Honey, are you okay?"

Julia stirred slowly from her deep slumber, pain hitting her hard as she lifted her head off the pillow. She had forgotten for one blissful moment about her headache.

"Oh, God!" she impulsively called out. The pain was so overwhelming. She reached for her head as she laid it back down on the pillow. Julia covered her eyes with the small blanket she had borrowed from Thomas. Her stomach turned and she felt suddenly nauseated, so she was careful to stay extremely still. Even breathing felt awful.

"Tom, is that you?" Julia asked into the air while wincing in pain. Her eyes remained closed and she didn't necessarily even want an answer. Any movement seemed to hurt.

Then she remembered this morning's terrible events with their son. She groaned aloud.

"Yeah, honey," replied Tom. "What's wrong? Are you sick or something?"

"Yes. I have a horrible headache. What time is it?"

"It's only 2:45; I just came home to grab something I forgot. I can stay if you want me to?"

"You can?" asked Julia, in puzzlement. Here, she had been whining to herself for hours about him not helping. She couldn't believe he had just offered.

"Wait, what about work?"

"Well, I probably shouldn't take time off since it's my first week there. But, if something is really wrong and you need help, I'll stay."

"No. Just go back to work," she replied, with a defeated sigh.

"But, honey, you don't look good." he pointed out with concern, "I mean, you have Thomas' blanket on your head."

"I do?" Julia said, lifting the blanket off her eyes to look at what had been on her head, for probably hours. It had comforted her through the afternoon.

"No, it's okay," she told her husband. "I'll be fine. I just need to sit up and wake up a little. The kids will be getting off the bus soon from school. I need to be awake."

"Okay, if you're sure. Sorry about your headache." Tom leaned down to give his wife a kiss on the head. He hesitated, but then turned and shut the back door behind him.

Julia could hear his car start and pull away.

"Oh, wow." she thought, still holding her head and her son's blanket against it for relief.

Julia pulled herself up from their floral print couch and when she came to her senses, she fell back down to the couch, realizing she missed a huge opportunity. She forgot to tell Tom about Kyle.

THE NEXT MORNING

The sun is shining brightly through my window and peeking through the curtains as my eyes flutter open to a new morning. When I wake, I'm lying on my back just like I had been the night before. The image of the strange, ghostly creature hovering near my ceiling fresh in my mind. *What the heck was that?*

Remembering nothing else of last night's events, other than being hit by an unknown object from the misty entity above my bed, I start to sit up when a jolt of pain hits my forehead. I cry out, grabbing the painful area with my hand. It feels like my head was hit by a bolt of lightning and split in two.

"Oh my, God!" I'm disoriented and panicked when I twist around in my bed sheet, mistaking it for an attack by some unknown creature.

I flail around my bed fighting this unknown person who seems to be restraining me, but soon realize I can't see!

I can't see!

Tangled in a heap, I end up too close to the edge of my bed and tumble to my bedroom floor.

I manage to get one of my legs out from under my bed sheet and have a split second to brace myself for the impact, hitting my bottom and lower back.

"Ow!" I yell, just as my mother runs into my room.

"Becca?! What happened to you?"

"Mom?" I rub my eyes trying to focus, but I can't see her. All I see is a blur of colors. It's like watching a scary television show when the television editors blur the screen for effect.

"It's me, Becca." She walks up behind me as I lie on my bedroom floor and puts her arms around me, lifting me, "Now, let's get you up."

Now back on my bed sitting with my legs dangling down, I grasp the edges to secure myself, afraid of falling.

This really scares my mother. I think she finally realizes something is really wrong.

"Tell me what happened, Bec," she asks with concern.

"I don't know!" I say with fear. "Last night I woke up to this white mist above my head and ..." I trail off trying to remember what happened.

"Something white was above your head last night?"

"Yes! And then it threw something at me!!" I pause for a moment hearing how crazy I must sound. "I think." I say. "I, I can't remember anything after that."

My mother stands near me, supporting me as I sit on the bed confused as ever.

"Wait, I remember seeing a face."

Not really wanting to recall the terrifying sight, I start telling my mother, "Its face turned from a pretty, child-like face to an evil, menacing face. Then I saw a dark object come from its arm and everything went black.

"Now, all I know for sure is that my head hurts!" I say as I grab my head, pain still coursing across my forehead.

"Then I got stuck in my bedcovers and fell out of bed trying to get loose but, but, I ..."

"Honey?" my mother's voice interrupts my thoughts. She clearly sees I'm overwhelmed.

"Mom, I can't see!" I yell. "Everything is blurry! I can't see you!"

****

It is 9:30 a.m. and my mother calls our doctor and takes the day off work. She helps me into her shiny, light-blue Cougar inside our garage. Then I struggle to put on my seat belt.

Luckily, most of my vision has come back and I can see objects again, though other things are still slightly hazy. To say I'm very glad to be able to see again is an understatement. I noticed it starting to improve when my mother helped me to get dressed. It keeps getting better.

According to my mother, I have a huge welt on the right side of my forehead. She insists it looks like a hardboiled egg sticking out of my head.

I panic and want to see it, but she won't let me look, saying, "It's best if you don't look. Just let the doctor look; seeing it will just cause you more stress.

"I can't help you unless you calm yourself down, Becca," she tells me. So, I take a few deep breaths like she's told me before to try to ease my anxiety.

On our way to the doctor, I touch my forehead to feel the sore and wince in pain. *Maybe I don't want to see it.*

"Becca, don't touch it!" my mother snaps at me. "It's not good to touch it. There is nothing we can do until we see the doctor. I don't know what you did last night or this morning, but this is insane," she states with frustration.

Great, we're back to her not believing me. Who could make this up?

"Mom, I told you what happened last night and this morning!" I cry to her. "How come you never believe me?"

"Becca, I just know you. You have an active imagination. It was probably just an active dream and this morning you accidently fell out of bed. So please just calm down."

"Wow ..." I say, taken aback by her remarks.

"What?" she asks me a few moments into my silence, as I quietly take in her hurtful remarks.

"Nothing. You will never listen so there is no point in speaking to you." I just look out the window seething with pain and anger from her harsh statement.

With a small sigh, my mother shakes her head as we pull into Dr. Brenton's office parking lot and park the car.

****

"Well, I'll say!" responds Dr. Brenton to the large lump sticking out of my forehead.

"What?" my mother questions at his remark. "What is it, Dr. Brenton?"

"Well, I really don't know how this could have happened as you explained it," he says. Dr. Brenton has been our doctor since I was four years old. His daughter and I went to Catholic school together and I've spent a lot of nights at their house. Needless to say, my mother really trusts his opinion.

"What do you mean?"

"Well Mrs. Fletcher, you describe Becca falling out of her bed this morning, but this injury could only have come from an object striking her head from above."

"What?" My mother responds, as she covers her mouth with her hand trying to hide her shock.

"Yes, look right here," he says taking his finger and tracing the swelling bulge on my forehead, which is a nice shade of purple and black now. "Whatever struck Becca's head must have been large to cause this size bump. Also, I see no other way to say this, but given the location of her injury, the blow had to have come from something striking her hard from above the head."

We just sit for a minute, processing what Dr. Brenton has evidently pointed out. *At least I feel justified.* My mother's face tells me she's thinking about how she can disprove the doctor's theory, but she apparently comes up with nothing.

Sensing this, he continues, "Now you see, if she had fallen like you said and hit her head, logically it would have struck her on the face somewhere. But this knot is high on the right side of her forehead in the front.

"Also consider that you said you found Becca sitting on her bedroom floor. If she had fallen and struck her head on her bed on the way down, then she would mostly likely have landed face down, not on her bottom. So again, everything points to your daughter being hit with an object from above."

"That's what I said!" *Finally, someone on my side!*

"Was there anyone else in the house at the time who could have done this?" asked the doctor in a serious tone.

"No," my mother answers. "It was just me, Becca, and Zander, of course. As far as I know everyone slept through the night.

"You said someone struck you, correct Becca?" he asks.

"Yes. I don't know what it was, but I woke up in the middle of the night and this weird mist-like shape was over my bed. It changed form into an evil face. Then after a few minutes, it threw a black thing at me. I don't know where it came from or what it was or where it went after it hit me. But that's what happened! I don't remember anything after that. My memory just goes blank."

"Well, that is an important piece of information," Dr. Brenton says, addressing both my mother and I. "If Becca were hit hard with a blunt object, she could temporarily lose her sight. That is another symptom of a concussion. So, Becca," he starts, as he turns toward me and reaches onto his left upper pocket and pulls out a tool with a light on it. "You are one lucky lady to even be alive, with the way that object hit you." He continues with the exam as he speaks, looking at my eyes with his light. Then he stops to look at my expression. "Be thankful!"

"And you're lucky she's alive too, Mom." he says, addressing my mother this time and giving her a calming smile.

"We could have lost her. A hit like that just an inch in one direction or the other, could have had devastating results," he says, taking out his stethoscope and telling me to breathe in and out slowly.

"Well, my dears," he speaks, as he gears up to end his session with us. "It looks like all is okay now. Put some ice on that injury three times a day. It will help with the swelling. No hot showers or baths for a while. Also, Mrs. Fletcher," he says facing my mother. "Don't let her sleep until at least 11p.m. tonight. She could have a concussion. I'd rather be safe than sorry. I'm sure you want to be as well," he says and nudges my mother's upper arm with a smile.

"Thank you. Ice, no shower or bath, no sleep. Got it," replies my mother, as my doctor walks over to the sink and washes his hands, preparing to go.

"Okay, young lady, you are good to go!" he says enthusiastically, as he dries his hands. I sit in shock on the tall patient bed in the middle of the examination room.

That's it?? I almost died!

"Becca, I'm not kidding. No sleep until 11 p.m. and take care of yourself."

****

You would think that after my doctor's visit, my mother would finally listen to me about what I saw and the happenings in the house, but no. I beg her to listen to me, but she just turns a deaf ear.

One night I couldn't stand it anymore. I come out of my room after not being able to sleep, all of the traumatic incidents on my mind. I walk down the hallway. She's laying with her feet up on the long blue velvet couch and a pillow behind her back to prop her up, so she can see the television. *Frasier* was on.

When I get closer, I can tell she already knows what I want to say, and she definitely doesn't want to hear it, but I have to get it off my chest. So, I just start talking about the sounds in the house day and night, about Mrs. Walter, and about everything I have seen over the past 6 years.

But she still doesn't want to hear it, "I said, I don't want to talk about it, Becca! I mean it. STOP!"

However, I can't stop. I want to finally let it out. "But Mom," I say, "what if Mrs. Walter showed herself to me in order to get help?"

"Oh, my God, Becca!" she yells back at me. "I said STOP!!"

Seeing her reaction, I know there's no use. So, I hang my head, turn around, and walk to my bedroom – that I'm completely terrified of.

The house is so quite now, that I can hear my mother sigh from the couch as I walk away. She is upset and doesn't want to face the truth.

I step into my cold bedroom and start to close the door, but leave my light on because now I'm scared to death of the dark. *Thanks to the creepy mist!*

I start to close my door but hesitate. *Maybe she will realize that what I said is important and come down the hall to see me and offer some help. All she has to do is call our church!*

I mean, St. Patrick's in Troy was Mrs. Walter's church, too. A priest can come over and bless the house and tell Mrs. Walter she is free to move on and go to heaven! She was Catholic! She has to listen! My thoughts are more hopeful, but I know my mother and it's really no use. *She'll never listen.*

Suddenly my thoughts turn to other bad things. I can't help but feel hopeless, as I lay awake in bed. I feel like all this is my fault. I feel terrible for having Lexi at the party, knowing she brought an evil presence into my house making it even worse. I can't believe it! The house is even scarier than it already was before! Some friend she is!

****

The following Monday at school does not go well. I feel so lost, like my best friend moved away.

My mother found out what happened at the party,

and also heard from another parent over the weekend that Lexi got caught stealing a bathing suit from the mall. Something I thought she was doing but had no proof of. Now she's finally been caught.

My mother tells me Sunday night that I am not allowed to see or speak to Lexi again, though I have already decided that.

Mom really freaks out when I tell her about Lexi's father, too, and the séance and how Lexi planned it all out.

"Becca. Birds of a feather flock together! Do you really want someone to think you are like Lexi?" she asks me. "Stealing things from stores and holding séances in people's houses?"

My mother's words hit me like a bolt of lightning, and I know she's right.

"No, I don't want people to think of me like that, Mom," I plop down on the blue couch in our family room with a sad sigh. *Do people think that of me since I was hanging out with her?*

"I know you don't," she confirms. She places her hand on my shoulder to comfort me.

"I know you wouldn't want others to think that way about you, honey, because you are a good person." This time she looks at me and puts her hand under my chin, lifting it toward her to better see my face. "I know that because I raised you to be that way. Lexi isn't good to you and you deserve a friend who will be good to you."

"I know," I reply, still sulking a little.

"I know it's hard. Sometimes people aren't good to us or aren't good for us and we don't understand it, and it's hard to let them go, even when we know it's best. But Becca, it is best, and in time, you will make another friend who will be good to you. Lexi has A LOT of problems that you don't need!"

"Yes, Mom."

Taking comfort from my mother's words, on Monday I go into school and act the same as usual in the morning, as I wait with Lexi for the first morning bell. In order not to upset her I decided to not say that I cannot speak to her anymore or be friends. Instead, I decide on a plan to taper off with time, so it's less noticeable.

Lexi is scary! Who knows what she would do to me if she found out I can't be friends with her anymore and that my mother told me she found out everything. It's just better this way. I don't like disobeying my mother's direct order of breaking things off with her, but I feel it's safer this way. Like I said, Lexi is crazy. I was afraid of her. *Look at how she treated me when we were friends!*

Everything was going well. I was acting like everything was completely normal. Until Emily comes around the corner in the hallway outside the cafeteria and blurts out, "I thought you weren't allowed to talk to Lexi anymore!" Emily says it directly to me, overlooking Lexi nearby, like she can't hear or see her. "Didn't your mother say you couldn't be her friend anymore?"

I freeze and stare at Emily in a, "how could you say that," kind of face. Then I turn back to Lexi to explain and talk it over with her; however, Lexi decides to kick me in my right side, and I hit the floor. As she looks down at me, I see her face fill with hate and anger, and I swear a tiny hint of loneliness. My mom was right!

Lexi turns and walks down the hallway. I never see or speak to her again.

THE END IS NEAR

Julia woke up to a beam of sunlight streaming in through her new home's bedroom window. It was a foggy, damp January morning. She heard a car horn beep behind her house, which helped wake her. She turned over to see her clock. It was 6 a.m.

Julia turned her body over the rest of the way, moving her hand to her husband's pillow to wake him. His alarm must not have gone off this morning and he'll be late, she thought. But Tom wasn't there. His pillow and side of the bed were empty as Julia swept her arm and hand around, searching for her husband.

"Tom?" she called out, slowly sitting up and feeling the haziness of sleep wear away. "Oh, my God ..." she mumbled, as she brought her hands to her temples in pain. Julia's headache had not subsided with the night's rest.

"Ugh!" cried Julia, in frustration from the pain.

"Mom?" called out Sara, as she entered her bedroom.

"What is it, Sara?" Julia replied sharply to her daughter's calls. Sara, who had been walking down the hall heard the unusual hostility in her mother's voice and stopped short before her mother's bedside. Then she took a step back in confusion.

"Mom? Are you okay?"

"Hi, dear," responded Julia, as she reached out blindly to her daughter, feeling guilty over her negative outburst. Embracing Sara in a positive morning hug and half smile while her head pounded inside, Julia tried to pretend she was fine to not worry her young daughter.

For days, Julia tried everything to eliminate stress, which is what the doctor she had seen last week said was her biggest problem. It was either that or seasonal allergies and since it was winter, stress seemed to be the most reasonable cause, especially considering the recent move and all the trouble she had been experiencing with Kyle!

Julia had tried hot baths, teas, and even honey. If it were allergies or a cold, she couldn't get rid of it. Then she tried taking walks to feel better.

Maybe some sort of exercise! That would help she thought, but it was too cold outside! Who wants to walk outside in Ohio in January? The cold air agitated her headache and made it worse. She felt hopeless and feared the pain would never go away.

"How are you this morning, honey?" she asked Sara, as she continued to hug her close and rub her temples at the same time.

"Fine." Sara looked at her mother in despair. "Mom, really, are you okay?" asked Sara with concern.

Julia sighed, sat up, and took a deep breath. "Yeah, hon. My headache just won't go away, that's all," responded Julia, as she looked her sweet little girl's eyes.

"Okay," Julia said, as she stood up from bed and took Sara's hand. "Let's get ready for school! Okay?"

"Okay," agreed Sara, as Julia led her back to the bedroom to pick out some clothes for the day.

****

Brrrriing, brrring… came the sound of the telephone interrupting Julia's slumber. It was 1 p.m. and the kids were in school, so Julia took advantage of some alone time and tried to get some rest to feel better. It must have done the trick, because she felt better when she woke. Maybe her headache finally had calmed down.

"Who is that?" Julia said aloud to herself impatiently. Suddenly a streak of dread entered her mind. *Oh, no!* She remembered the last time she had gotten a call in the middle to the day. She recalled Kyle's principal calling to tell Julia to pick Kyle up, because he had pulled the school's fire alarm.

OH God. … I can't handle another thing. She thought becoming more impatient.

For the past few days Kyle came and went as he pleased, and Julia let it go. She figured it never worked when she tried to control him, so she might as well ignore it for a little while and get herself better first. Meanwhile, she called a few psychiatrists, but only heard back from one so far and he didn't take their insurance. So now she was waiting to hear back from the others. She knew something had to be done and soon. Her throbbing migraines were high on the list of reasons she didn't want to answer the phone. One. More. Thing!

"Hello," Julia spoke into the phone.

"Hello, is this Mrs. Walter, mother of Kyle Walter?" asked the voice on the other end of the phone. Julia unfortunately recognized the man's voice. It was Kyle's principal, Mr. Seekins.

"Yes, what did he do now?" Julia openly asked, with a lack of emotion that she should have been ashamed of. But instead, she just slumped backward into the couch still holding the phone to her ear and stretching the cord to reach.

Julia's blunt question clearly caught him off guard and he stumbled a little before answering. "Well, Mrs. Walter, Kyle was found wandering the halls during class time, and when he was asked why, he simply told the teacher, that he 'didn't care about class and hated school, so why bother?'"

"Lord," mumbled Julia under her breath, fed up enough with the situation to not care if the principal heard her or not.

"Sorry. Mrs. Walter," replied Mr. Seekins. "What did you say?" asked the principal trying to play dumb and act like he hadn't heard her correctly. But Julia didn't care; she was over it.

"I'll be there when I can." Julia hung up the receiver, without a goodbye or another word.

****

Julia drove to Kyle's school and parked her car just as the school buses were beginning to pull up. She stepped out of her car, crossed traffic, and waited for two buses to drive by her and then she slowly walked into the school. She let out a frustrated loud puff of air as she pulled the building door open.

She dreaded the whole conversation she was about to have with Mr. Seekins – again – because, the truth was, she didn't understand her own child. Her son clearly did not care about her, himself, or anyone else. Julia didn't understand where she had gone wrong and felt lost about what to do. Everything she tried, everything Tom tried, wasn't working; Kyle ended up cursing at them or walking out of the house, regardless of whether it was day or night. Julia had been through enough. All she figured she could do to avoid the worst at this point was to let him go and do his thing until she heard back from a psychiatrist for help. She was ready to throw her hands in the air and give up.

After Julia walked into the school, she headed straight into the main office and saw Kyle sitting on a bench near the principal's office slumped over and chewing gum without emotion. She walked right by him without saying a word and into Mr. Seekins' office.

"Mrs. Walter!" cried Mr. Seekins, as he quickly stood up. "We've been waiting for you."

"Well I'm here," replied Julia, as she quickly sat down and waited for the lecture.

"Mrs. Walter, are you alright?" Mr. Seekins asked as he took in her appearance and mannerisms while taking his seat behind the desk again.

"Yes," she replied with annoyance. "Look, I won't beat around the bush; I just don't know what to do!" Julia swiftly said, throwing her hands up in the air. "The kid takes off and does whatever the hell he wants, whenever the hell he wants! He won't take punishments and he yells and curses at us. I give up, Mr. Seekins!" She was holding back tears. "I do. I give up!" her voice strained and her spirit exhausted with despair and regret.

Julia was on the verge of crying. She knew if the tears started, they might never stop.

Plus, Julia didn't want to be that mother! The mother who cried in her kid's principal's office. The mother who couldn't help her child. The mother with a child out of control. It all hit her at once; she felt hopeless and desperate and knew she wasn't able to fix her son.

Suddenly Julia knew her worst fear as a parent had come true. She was that mother and there was nothing she could do. She wanted to die.

THE KEYS

Saturday night and I finally get Zander to bed. It takes almost two hours! It started with a late bath because I was finishing housework and trying to straighten up before my boyfriend, Kevin, came over. It's 1997 and now I am 17 years old with my first serious boyfriend. I'm so happy because the whole family really seems to like him, even my sister! She's really hard to please. So, it's exciting. I am so happy he's coming over tonight. It's really nice that he lives in the same neighborhood, but sometimes, like now, I wish it took him just a little longer to get here.

Kevin lets himself in and sets up the movie he rented for us from Kroger. A rom-com. I sit down on the couch and let myself sink in, letting out a long-deserved sigh of relief, then scoot over so I can snuggle into my favorite spot slightly under his arm. He hugs me like I knew he would, gives me a quick kiss, then presses "play" on the VCR remote.

"You know, Zander probably didn't want to go to bed because he knew I was coming over."

"Yeah, I know. He mentioned that. Several times." Kevin and I laugh because we are well aware that Zander prefers hanging out with Kevin and he isn't shy about letting him know it. He loved his big sister but having an older boy in the house wasn't something he was used to since he lived with two women. So, when Kevin is here, he always wants to be around and tries to get Kevin to play with him. And, as if on cue, Zander comes running out of his bedroom right then!

"Let me watch the movie with you!" cries Zander as he stands in front of us near the blue couch. "PLEASE…!" He begs me, putting his two hands together and to his chest in a plea like he's praying.

"Oh, my God!" I squeal with fright as Zander pops out from the hallway and scares me to death. "No."

"Then just let me play with Kevin a little while. PLEASE…!

"No."

"How about I just say 'Goodnight, buddy?'"

"Nooo..!" cries Zander as I stand up, take his hand, and begin walking him back to his bedroom for the night.

"You're going to bed!"

"No, Becca. I'm thirsty."

Oh, my God. "Go to your room and I'll get some water and bring it to you!" I tell him sternly.

That was the argument every time Kevin was near– "the water stall." He pretends to want water so he can stay up longer. This time I'm not falling for it. As I see Zander make his way down the hallway back to his room, I get him a small glass of water from the kitchen and start walking with it to his room.

"I won't be but a minute, Kevin. Sorry," I say, passing my boyfriend on the couch and walking down the hall.

Once Zander is finally in bed again, I come back and sit on the couch with Kevin and we begin the movie. After a while, I realize how nice it is to finally have Zander asleep, so I can relax a little.

While the movie's intro music plays, Kevin looks at me and I know what's coming. It's almost 9 p.m.

and I've been anticipating this all day. He moves in for another kiss and I lean in to meet him.

Then…

Jingle, jingle, …

"What was that?" I sit up, hating to leave my perfectly cozy spot, and give Kevin the same confused look that he is giving me.

"I don't know, but it sounded like it was in the kitchen."

Kevin pauses our movie. We look around the family room and don't see anything by the television or fireplace. We don't notice anything around the cut-out into the kitchen either.

"I don't see anything. Maybe something just fell off the counter."

"I guess," I say, before leaning back into him and the couch, while he restarts the movie.

Booooom!

Kevin and I jump off the couch at the same time and see Zander running down the hall.

"Mommy!!" he squeals, as he runs past us toward the kitchen.

"Mom?" Zander stops near the kitchen table and looks around for our mother. His little eyebrows draw together and his head tilts to the side. Clearly he's as confused as we are. He glances around the kitchen once more but doesn't find what he's looking for. … what we're *ALL* looking for.

"Zander!" I call to my confused brother, as I make my way to the kitchen to meet him. He's just standing, frozen right there in the middle of the kitchen in puzzlement.

"Where's Mommy? I heard her!" he adds, his face obviously sad with disappointment as he continues searching the kitchen and family room. "You did?" Kevin and I ask in unison.

Walking over to Zander I lean down and give him a quick hug to ease his fears. I'm not sure if he needs comfort or if I do, but the hug seems to work for both of us.

"Awww." My voice cracks as I empathize with my little brother, his pitiful bottom lip sticking out and his face growing sadder by the minute as he takes in my pity and wants more. I squeeze him tighter. *I can't help it; the kid is SO CUTE!!*

"I heard her keys!" Zander insists, his feet stomping on the floor.

"You did?" I glance over my shoulder at Kevin, who is sitting on the couch watching the whole unbelievable scene unfold.

"Yeah, didn't you?" he asks, still looking a bit pitiful but also confused.

A speechless, "Oh" forms on Kevin's lips.

"Where'd you hear keys, Zander?" Kevin asks.

Pointing toward the table, he replied, "Right over there. When she gets home, Mom always puts her keys on the table. And that's what I heard. So, where is she?" Zander demands. Those big sad eyes just stare up at us begging for an answer we can't supply.

"He's right. She does that every day. ... walks in and immediately puts her keys down on the table."

"Well kiddo, we don't know what the noise was and I'm sorry, but it wasn't your mom's keys. She isn't home yet."

Zander hangs his head, clearly disappointed at the news. And I was about to deliver another blow. He has to go back to bed.

"Ok, Zander. Back to bed. Sorry, Mom's not home,

but it is way past your bedtime! Go ahead and give Kevin a hug if you want and tell him goodnight," I say, hoping that being allowed to have a moment with Kevin will ease the transition.

"Nooo!" Zander says. His frustration is obvious as he crosses his arms across his chest, and stomps on the floor.

"I know, but you have to listen to your big sister," I hold my hand out for him to take and, thankfully, he does.

I lead him back to his bedroom and hear no more protesting. He easily jumps back in bed and I tuck him snugly in. I think this time he's really tired, probably from all the excitement. "I'm sorry," I tell him again.

"I know."

I gave him another kiss goodnight on his forehead and tuck his stuffed dinosaur in with him, then stand to leave. "Night, night little guy. Mom will be home soon, and you'll get to see her in the morning, okay."

"Okay," he replies, as he yawns and closes his eyes. By the time I get to the door, he is already asleep.

I turn off his bedroom light, close his door, and make my way back to Kevin on the couch. And sit down when...

Jingle, jingle ... Comes the small metal sound again.

"You heard it again too, didn't you?"

Kevin shushes me. We both stand still listening but don't hear anything more.

"That was so strange. I'm starting to freak out a little. There have been so many weird sounds and visions I can't explain. Sometimes I think I'm going crazy!"

"I get it. Let's see if we can figure this one out for now."

We walk back to the kitchen to check out the table

again. We look around the kitchen and under the table, looking all around to find something, anything, that explains what we are hearing.

Maybe Mom is home! I walk toward the garage door inside the small kitchen. Kevin follows, and we both peek our heads out into my empty garage.

Nothing…There is no explanation.

Kevin and I look at each other as we both shrug our shoulders in defeat. Then we look at the table again where we thought the sound came from, trying to process what is happening.

"Bizarre …"

****

We finally have a chance to settle in and watch the movie. Lights out, we eat two bags of buttery popcorn and try to forget the jingling incident.

The movie's great and perfect for our night in. The lead male character pretends to dislike the woman the entire movie, irritating her every chance he gets. Fast forward ninety minutes, he shows up on her doorstep and breaks it to her that he's in love with her. He rambles on about all the reasons he admires her, the reasons he wants to spend the rest of his life with her, and the reasons he fought falling in love with her for so long. Of course, it was every woman's dream movie because we all want to hear this. Kevin was probably bored, but he didn't show it.

Kevin takes the hint from my good mood after the movie and bends down once more to kiss me. It doesn't take me long to pull him closer, fully engaging both of us in the kiss. *Watching movies at home is the best.*

The popcorn from the green glass bowl falls onto

the floor as it slips off my lap, forgotten.

Jingle, jingle, ...

Startled, we break our kiss and look at each other but don't pull away. Too scared to budge. We peek toward the kitchen table half expecting to see my mother standing there looking at us in disgust, in trouble for our kiss.

But we don't see her. The kitchen is dark, except for a dim nightlight coming from above the old stove. No shadows, no footsteps, no keys. Nothing.

"Oh, my God," says Kevin, shocked as he looks back at me. I can see the fear start in his eyes. He flips on the nearby lamp, but it doesn't reveal anything.

"I don't get it. Where is it coming from?" he's really frustrated now.

I let out a long sigh. This is more than some jingling keys and Kevin has no idea. I've kept this house's secret as long as I can and just hope the truth doesn't make him run.

"Kevin, I have to tell you something." Quite the understatement. *Something incredibly scary that will freak you out beyond your wildest nightmares, so please don't run.*

I begin to I spill my guts right there on the family couch. I tell him about all that I've seen growing up in the house – seeing Mrs. Walter and the odd sandwich making incident, the cold drafts, the knocks on the doors, stuff falling off my dresser, my horrible sweet-sixteen party and séance with Lexi, and the sickening misty white stuff. I tell him about my head injury and what Dr. Brenton said about how the object having had to come from above, and my mother's reactions.

I tell him *EVERYTHING!*

Kevin stays. He's as still as a statue, but he stays and doesn't run. I breathe a sigh of relief. However, I see his eyes are popping out of his head and his mouth is gaping open. I'm not sure he's breathing. I feel more confident. It feels good to get it off my chest! And bad at the same time.

Good and bad. I don't know! My brain is swirling. Swirling from bringing it all up, yes, but also because of what Kevin might think of me. *Will he dump me now? Will he think I'm crazy? Will my worst fear come true?*

God knows I've been tormented, about how all of these experiences are at odds with every Catholic belief I've ever had. Right now, the combo was giving me a throbbing headache that I didn't have time for. *But for now, I'll save my guilt for another day.* First, I need to deal with Kevin and see if we can move forward.

"Wait," Kevin says, as he holds up his hand to me. "Mrs. Walter?"

"Yes."

"Oh, I remember her!"

"You do?" I hadn't pieced together that he has lived in this neighborhood his whole life – regardless of who has lived in this house. And that he might have known or interacted with her. And I certainly didn't fathom he wouldn't blink an eye about the chaos that's been happening here tonight and how strange all this is. *But if he wants to skim over the fact that it sounds crazy, I'm good!*

"Yeah, a little. I can picture her anyway."

"What was she like?" I have to ask. I probably sound a little too excited to discuss the deceased, but I am so curious. I have to know. I need more information. *Had it been Mrs. Walter making us the sandwiches?* Mrs. Martin seemed to think so, but she was the only person I talked to about this until now. This might change everything and prove it was Mrs. Walter!

"Well, from what I recall, she looked like you

described, down to the clothes and make-up. I don't know if that's good or bad, but it sure sounds like her."

I don't know what to say. But I need a minute to process. My elbows go to my knees and my head follows. I sit silently with my head propped in my hands. I don't know how long I stayed like that before I looked up at Kevin again. *How can that even be? Dead people don't just appear like that. What do I do? Call the church? Tell my mother? We know how that would go. Keep quiet and hope nothing else weird happens? I always feel so lost and out of control with these situations. I'm only 17 for crying out loud! This shouldn't be bestowed on me! It's not fair!!*

Finally looking up at my boyfriend, relieved to find out after my strange reaction and all this weirdness that he's still there and looks so kindly toward me. I can't help but smile.

"I am a bit freaked out," he says, "but we'll figure it out," Kevin says, as he glances back at the kitchen with concern.

"Freaked out sums it up," I say, with a sarcastic half smile. "Try living here!'

"But, the key sound? That's new?" he asks.

"Yes, that's new," I tell him confidently with a concerned shoulder shrug as he rubs my knee to try to comfort me, and we both stare into the kitchen.

****

After that night, the jingling starts each night precisely at 9. Zander always comes running out of his room expecting to see our mom, but never finds her. It's crushing. He gets so upset each time, and I need to start all over again putting him back to bed. He's always so disappointed; it breaks my heart. The sound is nothing but a cruel joke!

Why is this happening and why won't it stop? I get so frustrated.

On the fourth night at 9, we both walk into the kitchen and again find no one there. By now, we are getting used to the sound and Zander doesn't get too upset.

I walk him back to his room and put Zander in bed, hoping he stays asleep, and then walk to my bedroom. I sit down at my desk to get some homework done, when I hear someone walking down the hallway.

Unalarmed, because Mom could have gotten home while I was putting Zander to bed, I barely glance up. My door is shut, so the light doesn't shine down the hall and give Zander a reason to stay up. *It'd be nice if Mom came in to see me and say goodnight.*

But nothing else happens. I watch my door and wait for the knob to turn, fully expecting it to. Waiting. And waiting…

No one comes in. No one even seems to be in the hall anymore.

Okayyy… I think to myself. Back to homework then.

An hour or so goes by, when I heard a familiar noise ring through the house.

Jingle, jingle, …"

It is loud this time!

Taking a minute to come up with a plan, I sit and look toward my door. I take a big breath in and let it out slowly to stay calm. My adrenaline is kicking in and I don't want to give it more attention. *Somehow that seems worse. If I just ignore it…*

My curiosity gets the better of me. I slowly stand up and walk to my bedroom door and just stand in front of it, waiting for someone to come in. *Maybe my mother is ACTUALLY home!!*

I hope.

Or is it another trick?

As I contemplate leaving my room, I hear them again! Footsteps coming down the hall toward my room!

Oh my God!

I start to panic. My palms are sweaty and my heart races so fast and loud that I half expect it to burst. Then the footsteps just stop.

Whatever it is, whoever it is, is right outside my door.

My chest heaves as I realize I don't have anything to protect myself with! I'm not giving up hope that it might legitimately be Mother, but what if it isn't!

I can't even protect myself, I'm weaponless. Suddenly my chest feels like it is going to collapse from fear. I realize I am in a bad situation. *How am I going to protect myself, or my little brother sleeping in the next room?*

Too late for that! My own thoughts don't help me stay calm, that's for sure.

I'm too stunned to grab anything, so I just stand there watching the doorknob.

Suddenly, I see the knob twist to the right in a slow motion, like whoever was holding it doesn't want to wake me or make a sound.

I take a step back and wait for the door to open, revealing the person behind it but it doesn't. Instead, the knob continues to slowly turn. It feels like the doorknob turns for an eternity until it *FINALLY STOPS*. It's twisted as far as it will go.

Now I'm nearly hyperventilating. I close my eyes and begin to pray quietly, "Please, God. Please, God help me!" I whisper over and over. When I open my eyes, the doorknob is in the same position, but the door stays closed.

Then, in one swift motion, whoever is on the other side of the door lets the knob go. The little brass doorknob springs back to its original position. No one comes in and I don't hear anyone walk away.

Taking in a deep breath, I stop to think.

What do I do now? I'm confused. I want to think before I react. It could make a big difference if someone is in the house.

My insides are racing like wind during a hurricane. I stay frozen in the same spot, while I listen for any more sounds, thinking of what to do.

If it was my mother, she would have come in. It obviously isn't her. *Who was it then?* I am over this! *What is happening in my house?*

After waiting and hearing no more sounds or signs of life in the house, I make the decision to check on Zander and search the house. Maybe it is him.

Taking in a huge breath for confidence, I grab the doorknob without holding back and in one swift motion, I turn the knob and pull the door open fast.

I look into the hallway. After a few seconds, my eyes adjust to the darkness of the hall with the light of my room still on behind me. I can see that the hallway is pitch black. There is nothing out of the ordinary. I hold my breath and listen before stepping out in the hallway.

I take one mini-step at a time and inch my way down the hall, until I reach Zander's room. I pop my head inside to see if he is okay. He looks undisturbed and tucked well into his dino-covers. He seems to be sleeping peacefully.

Continuing down the hall, nothing seems amiss. All is calm and quiet.

I walk through the rest of the house and nothing

seems out of place. I stand by the table and look around the kitchen and our family room, thinking to myself: *Who could this be? What is REALLY going on in here? I must be crazy?*

My thoughts soon fade, and I'm about to return to my bedroom to revisit homework when ...

Jingle, jingle, ...

Right where I stand! The key sound is so real! As if my mother's keys are physically hitting the wooden table right NOW, in front my eyes!

The only problem is there aren't any keys in sight and Mom isn't home.

WILL JULIA BE ALL RIGHT?

"Tom, you need to call the parts department. The floor manager says the machine on the floor is broken again and they can't find a part to fix it until Monday," Tom's secretary told him, as she quickly poked her head into his office, then dashed back to the phones.

"Not again!" grieved Tom, as he placed his head briefly in his hands and sighed. Taking a deep breath and pulling his hands away from his face, Tom lifted his office phone and put it to his ear. "Marcy!" Tom called out to his secretary. "Dial parts!"

"Hello," spoke the voice on the other end of the line.

"Yeah, Bob?" replied Tom. "What's all this about the machine parts? This is the third break down since I've been here. We have to get this reliably working, or we won't make our quota for the month. More importantly, we won't fulfill our customers' orders."

"I know, Tom," stated Bob. "To be honest, it's not looking good. These days parts are made so cheaply that they don't last like they used to."

"This is killing us! Can we get better quality parts from a different supplier?" Tom asked, more annoyed by the minute.

"Yeah. I've actually been working on a new contract. Let's get this situation straightened out, then maybe you and I can meet to go over future supply and maintenance plans. I'm sorry we haven't had a chance to get together since you started."

"Same here. That would be great. If you need anything from my end to get it done, just let me know." Truthfully, Tom's mind was a million miles from the tediousness of this whole parts/machine fiasco. If Bob would handle it on his own, that'd be fantastic.

God, it feels like I haven't seen my family in weeks! He couldn't even keep thoughts of his family at bay during work. There was no way around it – he was just plain worried. No, that didn't even come close to describing it! He was *beyond* worried about a family he hardly saw. *HIS* family. And even more so, Tom was seriously worried about his wife's well-being.

Oh, Julia. How are you really doing? He rubs his forehead to try to ease the stress. *Will she be all right?*

Tom had been working around the clock. All he did was work! He was never home for any family activities… for the important stuff. He would get home after 11 p.m. and lay down next to his already sleeping wife, trying not to wake her. Tom knew she needed sleep. But then he would be up and out the door in the mornings, before Julia or the kids even woke up, missing them all on both ends of the day. He couldn't keep this up. *None of them could.* In fact, he didn't know how much longer he could take it.

He was so stressed. Most of the time he didn't even stop long enough to eat. Sometimes he went days without lunch, only getting a bite if someone went out to get food for him. And he certainly never asked anyone to go. He couldn't do that in a new job.

Then in the evenings after a full workday, he often had meetings with clients – to keep new ones coming in and keep existing ones happy.

He loved working at Goodrich; he really did. But always being out with someone else's family was difficult.

Tom and a client would meet, and then he'd take them out for dinner and meet their families. He had to be the nice corporate businessman. And he was good at it! At least, he was good at it when his mind was in the game.

But lately, he couldn't help but think of how much he was missing his own family – how much he was missing out on their lives by not being together – and he really wanted to be having dinner with them, rather than with strangers.

And there was definitely an issue of Tom not taking care of himself properly. He was so fatigued. But that was going to have to take a back seat for a while.

Then there was his wife, Julia. It seemed that every time he saw her, she looked even worse! She was ill; he knew that. But why? And with what … he didn't know. And Tom didn't ask. He just tried not to upset her. She wasn't happy and she didn't seem to be sleeping well. She was sleeping a lot … but not well.

Tom knew things with Kyle weren't going well. He also knew Julia had likely given up on Kyle by now. And truthfully, she'd probably given up trying to talk to him too, because he was never home.

How can I help when I have to be at work? When I'm not home? Tom thought hopelessly. *God, I just want to be home! But as the man of the house, I'm responsible for bringing home the bacon.* To Tom, that was his lot in life: men worked to support their families, no matter what cost, and the women worked to raise their children. What could he say, this is the way it was. It's 1987, men worked. He had to pay the bills. *Who else is paying for those kids' colleges?*

We agreed on this before the kids were even born, so Julia understood him and why he was always gone. She was fine... right?

Tom had to believe Julia was fine, or that she would be soon. She normally ran the house like he did his job: with a good understanding of the problems and solid plans of action. She probably already had everything covered and Tom just hadn't been around to realize it.

Julia always had things under control. *When she is feeling ok.* Unfortunately, Tom had lost track of time in recent weeks and really hadn't checked in on her. But he needed to make a point of asking her. They needed to have a conversation so he could see for himself if Julia really was feeling better. If not, she'd need to go to the doctor. Tom stopped for a second to think. *She probably hasn't even looked for a new doctor since we moved.*

One thing was for sure – Tom needed to be *home*. The urgency of it was stronger than ever. Tom felt terrible.

Suddenly, he snapped back to reality when he heard Bob talking on the other end of the phone. *Right, parts.*

"Michigan is the only other place we could possibly get it, sir. But honestly, it will take about three weeks and I can't promise their parts will have a better performance than our current ones. But I've been researching it and have definitely heard more positive things about the Michigan supplier and the quality of their products," responded Bob. "I say we can give it a try." And with that final thought, the ball was in Tom's court.

"We really need to make this work. So, first, would you please finalize a plan for our immediate problem? It seems like you've already been investigating some solutions. Then, I want to have a sit-down and brainstorm. We need a plan to ensure our machines continue to work properly, including how we can ensure ongoing availability of quality parts for all our machinery in a timely manner."

Bob spoke up, "Then I say we order necessary parts from the usual supplier for our immediate needs. They'll be here in a day or two. And while things are up and running, we go ahead and order spare parts from Michigan. Hopefully, things will run smoothly, at least until they arrive." Bob continued, "This will ensure we will make it through, even if we run into another issue. And will allow the company to keep up with our incoming orders and continue to make our quotas for the month. It'll maintain our sales where they should be."

"Thanks, Bob. You have no idea what a relief it is to have you on top of this. You're a life saver. I realize it's what you do every day, but in the short time I've been here, you have never failed to come up with a solution. This perpetually malfunctioning machine is the perfect example. And it's not just that; I appreciate you. Goodrich definitely values your effort and teamwork. You're a real asset to the company." *And that's the truth!*

"Thank you very much, sir!" Bob replied back to his boss, with genuine enthusiasm. "I take pride in my work and really appreciate you noticing. I always try to work hard and really do love my job."

Tom could feel his heart pumping for the passion Bob had for his job. This was the part of his job that he loved. This is why he had relocated and wanted to move up the ladder with Goodrich. He moved with a company that had treated him well over the years. He enjoyed being able to collaborate with various departments and people to be able to fix issues and improve processes, to help the company grow. Not every person was a team player. And not every company valued teamwork, but his job fostered both and he couldn't have been more thankful.

"Bob, I assure you," stated Tom, to the prideful manager, "I will pass this along to your direct supervisor. If it hasn't been noticed before, I'm sorry. But details like this should be included in your annual performance review and be taken into account when discussing raises. You deserve it."

"Thank you very much, sir!" responded Bob gratefully. "You know, I have two kids going to college next year and every little bit helps."

"You do? I didn't know that. And two? Wow!"

"Yes, sir. Twins!"

Just the mention of kids had Tom thinking of his own family again and how he was neglecting them by being absent. He missed his wife and kids and felt guilty all over again. Yes, Tom sure did know that every little bit helped. And yes, he sure did love his job. He knew why he took it, why he stayed, and how much he had sacrificed to get where he was. But right now, he just hoped Julia and the kids were all right.

I pray this is all still worth it!

"Twins," Tom said again into the phone.

"Yes, sir. Um, sir, um ... Tom? Are you all right?"

THE SUICIDE

January 28, 1987

Julia walked into the pet store and asked the first clerk she saw where the dog leashes and collars were.

"Aisle three," directed the clerk pointing to the numbered aisle signs so she could find the items she was looking for.

"Thank you," replied Julia, as she walked toward the aisle indicated by the clerk. She found it easily and began looking at the dog collars and leashes that would soon take her life. *I just want it to be over, and over fast.* Julia searched through the seemingly endless choices and finally picked out four small dog collars, that were thin and black, and one long thin black dog leash.

As Julia approached the clerk at the checkout line, she smiled briefly at the young girl.

"Did you find everything you needed?" asked the young perky, blond teen, who seemed like a happy-go-lucky cheerleading type. Julia could smell her heavy scented floral perfume. For a moment Julia was jealous of how happy she was.

I used to be that happy. Not just when she was a teenager like the clerk, but in recent years with Tom and the kids. But then this move happened, and Kyle's behavior escalated into problems she couldn't solve alone. Now she didn't even have Tom to fall back on. *I never see my husband and I'm just a slave to my children! No one really cares about me.*

That was it. That summed up Julia's feelings. The sadness wasn't completely new, but it had been so completely constant lately, that she'd forgotten how to not feel depressed. *What does it feel like to be a person who isn't depressed?*

Nothing had changed since they moved. The kids still acted as if they didn't care about her – when they even acknowledged she was around. For the most part, they ignored her, unless they wanted something.

I don't have a purpose.

"Yes," she replied to the clerk, as she swiftly snapped back to her harsh reality.

"That'll be $44.57."

Julia reached into her tan, leather pocketbook and took out some cash to pay the too-perky clerk. She watched Ms. Happy fill the small white bag. This would be her last purchase – ever. Honestly, it was a relief that someone so happy and untainted was helping her through this process. A process that, thankfully, Ms. Happy was unaware of.

She gratefully accepted the bag filled with her fate, then turned, and left the pet store.

It was impossible to not reflect on how happy she was before this move. Tom removed her from the happiest place she ever lived, *my 2095 home in Troy,* Julia thought, as she walked out of the pet store to the parking lot, where her car awaited, *to Akron. Maybe other people liked it here, but not her, the only place she wanted to be was in Troy, Ohio. Her home, sweet home.*

I want to be in my family room, my kitchen, and my own bedroom. I want to walk the halls of the house I love and adore.

The house where I was happy. God, I miss it. Maybe this way, happiness will be waiting on the other side. There isn't any point in going on. I've been having this conversation with myself for too long now and it always ends the same. I can't help myself. I can't help Kyle. There is no point in continuing to try. My help isn't effective. My help isn't enough. My God, my help isn't even wanted! I just want it to be over.

And soon, it would be.

Julia pulled in the driveway of her small two-story white house. Putting the car in park, she unbuckled her seat belt and slowly stepped out of the car. "Bye car," she said aloud, to her little gold Ford Taurus. She looked around the inside one last time. So many memories in there. Family. Babies, little kids, big kids … car seats and feet kicking the back of my seat … ball practices, big games, church, vacations … spilled coffee and spilled juice. French fries between the seats, and coins everywhere. *Did someone lick the window?* Shopping, dinners, and girls' nights out. *My 2095 friends.*

She slammed the car door.

What does it matter? It's just an object. I can't take it with me! Julia walked into her garage and pushed the button to close door, before entering the house. As she walked into the kitchen entryway, she took off the winter coat Tom had bought her a couple years ago for Christmas. She gently draped it over the back of their wooden kitchen chair as usual and sat down.

Julia leaned over to grab the small white bag, that contained her fate and proceeded to dump the items out onto her wooden kitchen table.

For a moment, she sat at her table and just stared at the leash and collars. *This is it!* She thought. Julia felt like this was what she had been brought to. With no one listening, no one helping, and no one really caring, she didn't see another option. *What good am I?*

It always seemed like people knew when others needed help. Like someone would step up. Like someone would walk into her life and say, "I've got you." *Certainly the neighbors know I'm home alone, right? The 2095 neighbors would have.* She never saw Tom anymore – he worked all the time. Obviously. His car was never in the driveway! The stress of that alone was enough. How could he not know she needed help? How could he not step up?

Truth is, Julia just wanted to be happy, to be in a place she could *feel* happiness. *I want to be in the ONLY place I have ever been happy. Soon. I'll be there soon.* Julia told herself, as she mindlessly strung the black, thin dog collars together, finally fastening them to the longer black, thin dog leash. This was her fate.

Julia walked into the garage, with the fastened strand and located the ladder. She picked up the ladder and carried it across the garage, so that when it was opened, it was aligned with the attic door in the ceiling.

Then she climbed the ladder toward the little door. When she reached the attic, Julia grabbed the pulley to bring down the stairs from above. The stairs flowed down so easily toward her, *inviting her in.* As the attic stairs came down, she quickly jumped down beside the ladder, so she could push it out of the way and prevent a collision.

With the attic stairs descended, Julia drew in a deep, refreshing breath, and placed her right foot on the first step. She leaned inward toward the stairs, as she held on to the rails with both hands and looked up into the dark attic void, anticipating her next step. *Funny, I haven't been up in the attic since we moved here.*

Julia continued her oddly peaceful ascent up the attic

stairs, with full awareness of the dog leash and collars in hand. Looking for the light pull switch, she peeked through the darkness and waited for her eyes to adjust. Soon Julia spotted it and pulled down hard on the little string. The 40-watt bulb clicked on to dimly reveal the attic and its hidden contents.

Huh! Not much up here. As Julia scanned the small space, she noticed some old empty boxes from the previous owners. *Tom hasn't even put our stuff up here yet!* Frustration over him never being home was ever present and she let out a deep sigh.

Julia stepped up onto the last rung. She took the long black dog leash from her hand, that she had so carefully carried up with her and fastened it to the metal bracket at the top, that held the stairs in place. Then she cautiously turned her body to face forward, careful as to not fall. Julia quietly turned once more, looking out toward the closed garage door.

"Okay, this is it!" Her words echoed around the small attic, as Julia slipped the self-made noose over her head from behind and felt it tighten.

Then she jumped.

THE DOPPELGANGER EFFECT

Jingle, jingle comes the familiar sound of mom's car keys hitting our wooden kitchen table like clockwork, in the middle of the night. So loud it wakes me from a dream where I was endlessly bagging groceries for mean customers who wouldn't stop yelling at me. "You ruined my produce!" I recently started a new job as a bagger and cart collector for the store not too far from home, so the dream was not surprising.

"Wait!" I cry out, as I sit up after hearing the familiar sound. Flinging my feet out of bed, I jump into the fuzzy slippers I had just gotten for Christmas and slip out of bed. I grab my new pink terrycloth bathrobe and wipe the sleep from my eyes, as I head toward my bedroom door in the darkness.

Funny. The kitchen light is on. Maybe Mom really is home. I stop for a second to think. "What time is it?" I say out loud, while searching my room for the clock.

4 a.m.! Why is my mom up at this hour? It just doesn't make sense.

Turning back to my bedroom door, I open it, wait, and listen.

Bang, boom, bang, shuffle, shuffle, bang, boom! The noise ricochets through the small ranch.

It sounds like she is doing dishes, but that still makes no sense! I move down the hallway, which is dimly lit by the kitchen's light.

As I reach the end of the hall, I look around for my mother in the kitchen, but don't see anyone. I continue walking toward the kitchen and when I reach the table, I look around for my mother. The door to the garage opens and startles me so much, that I jump in the air and let out a small scream, "Agh!" I take my hand and hold my stomach, as the adrenaline releases from my veins making its way up from my legs to my stomach and eventually lands in my throat; I try to catch my breath and calm myself.

Mom's wearing her favorite turquoise sweater that was short on her waist, with little sewn-in pockets and a top to bottom stripe pattern in the fabric, with her worn in blue jeans.

"Mom! Oh my, God! You scared me to death!" I cry out as I see her – barely holding my stomach in check and catching my breath from the shock.

It doesn't take long to realize my mom still doesn't see me. No "sorry" or anything, which isn't like her. I stand up from where I was leaning on the back of a kitchen chair and look more closely. She seems mostly normal, but her expression is odd.

"Mom, are you okay?" I ask her. Mom looks at me strangely, almost through me, like she's never seen me before.

"Mom, are you feeling all right?" I say, as I step closer and reach out my hand to comfort her. I'm still trying to piece together what's happening.

Mom swiftly moves to avoid my touch by bending backward in a circular motion. Then she runs from the kitchen through the dining room. I can see that she looks scared.

"Mom!" I call out to her, as I hastily run after her. *What the heck is going on?*

I run through the small dining room following her, then around the bend to the small hallway leading into her bedroom, where I see her disappear into the darkness. I stop.

Standing near the open door to my mother's bedroom, I stay silent as my eyes adjust. I don't see any movement or hear a sound, which really freaks me out. *How can there be no movement at all? I saw her run in here.*

I take a step into my mother's bathroom and still don't see anyone or any movement. As I turn, I step toward my mother's bed. My mother is asleep in her bed! I take a few steps closer and see her chest rising and falling as if she's in a deep sleep. She is wearing her tan silk and lace nightgown she has had for years. I step closer and reach out to her. As my heart beats a thousand miles a minute, I touch her foot.

"Mom?" I say – not even recognizing my own voice.

"Becca?" Mom's voice clearly gives her away. She wasn't just running down the hall. She raises her head from the pillow to look at me. "What is it? Is there something wrong?"

"I don't know how to say this, but I just saw you in the kitchen. How did you get in here so fast and fall asleep?" I sound crazy even to myself!

"Becca, I don't know what you're talking about, but I got home from work hours ago and came right to bed. I didn't want to wake you and your brother." Mom rolled over away from me. "Now don't worry and go back to bed, honey. We can chat in the morning."

"But you were doing dishes!" I say, but it's no use. My mother is already asleep again.

Oh my, God! I can't believe this! How is it possible that I just saw my mother in the kitchen, and she acted like she didn't know me! Her own flesh and blood, and now she's suddenly been asleep this whole time! Was that even my mom in the kitchen? What on earth IS happening??

Also, what the heck was all that noise then that woke me up in the first place? And HOW could she possibly have been sleeping in her own bed for the past several hours? None of this makes any sense...

Crazy thoughts run through my head, as I stand beside my sleeping mother. I'm a shaky mess and afraid of walking to my bedroom alone and she's out cold!

Oh God ...

THE FRONT DOOR

Waking up to Gypsy barking, I turn my head to see my clock and see it's 4 a.m. – again, *What the heck is going?*

Pulling myself out of bed, I grab my slippers, bathrobe, and walk down the hall to see what the commotion is about. To my amazement, I step out of the hallway and turn toward the foyer to see our front door wide-open.

The wind is whirling around our small foyer from outside like a small tornado, as our tri-colored collie stands in a firm position right in front of our open front door furiously barking at thin-air, as if someone is there. But no one is there.

Soon, I see my mother walking down the small hallway from her bedroom, to also survey the scene.

"What the heck is going on?" she asks me, her face looking as confused and tired as mine.

"I don't know. I just came out to find her barking. She won't stop, and the front door was wide open!" I state, as we both turn and look back at Gypsy. "Did you leave the door open?" I ask my mother.

"No!" cries my mother in surprise. "You know I deadbolt it every night and put the key on the other side of the room."

True, my mother locks the door each night at 9:30 and places the key on a chair on the other side of the foyer because she's always afraid of someone breaking in. She thinks someone can punch through the side glass by the door, and twist open the deadbolt. She is extra cautious. She even bought a key lock. *How could the front door possibly unlock itself?*

"Okay, well how did this happen then?" I say.

"I don't understand it," replies my mother. "Gypsy!" my mother turns to our pet and tries to get her attention, so she will calm down. "Gypsy, baby! … "

But the dog won't break her trance, facing the air outside our front door. She won't stop barking. After trying a few times to get the dog's attention, my mother steps forward and closes the door, hoping the dog will just stop. Gypsy cries out as if someone has stepped on her tail or foot, alarming my mother, and causing her to stumble backward, as the door opens again. Then Gypsy bolts off into the night.

Mom and I rush to the wide-open door only to see Gypsy already clear down our street continuing to bark, as if she is chasing something.

"Well, this is going to be fun," says my mother to me sarcastically. "I guess I'll get the flashlight and go track her down." My mother walks into the kitchen and opens our junk drawer retrieving the flashlight. Then she goes to find her shoes in her bedroom.

As mom disappears into her bedroom, I peer outside and look down the street for Gypsy. I can no longer see her, but I can hear her barking getting further away.

"It sounds like she's past the end of our street now, Mom!" I shout to my mother.

"Well," she says, appearing behind me with her tennis shoes on and flashlight in tow, "I guess I'll follow her barking then. Our neighbors are going to love us in the morning," says my mother sarcastically.

"This is so strange ..." I say to her, as she heads out the door.

"Very strange, indeed."

For the next few months, it's the same scenario: my mother and I get woken up at 4 a.m., usually on a Wednesday, to our front door being blown wide open and Gypsy barking at the night air as if someone is there, but no one ever is.

Then Gypsy runs out the front door and down the street barking and my poor mother is forced to retrieve her at the far end of the street in the dark, wearing only her nightgown and tennis shoes, no matter the weather.

No one ever understands how the door opens by itself without a key.

****

One night I will never forget, I'm determined to find an answer! I set my alarm for 3:50 a.m. and get dressed. Walking drowsily down the hallway in my fuzzy pink slippers and bathrobe, I sat down in the cold black and metal chair that my mother always places the deadbolt key on every night. I wait, staring directly at the door. I know the door will open, and I'm determined to find out how it opens by itself so I can tell my mother.

For ten minutes I wait. Then suddenly I hear Gypsy start to move from her sleeping spot in front of my mother's room. She gets up as if in a daze, looking half asleep and trudging her way toward me. Like she knows something is about to happen.

For a moment I think maybe she was coming to see me to say hello. She's probably wondering what on earth I'm doing, sitting here alone and so late at night.

But she's not coming to see me after all.

Shifting her body weight still in her trance-like state, she faces the front door and begins to growl. I look at the side glass window near the door thinking she must see someone there, only to find no one.

Not a soul!

"Gypsy, honey," I say to her, trying to comfort her and calm her down. "There is no one there." But nothing seems to calm her.

So, I just sit, wait, and observe. Gypsy's head is low to the floor, as she continues to growl. It seems as if her growl-like voice is getting more intense, as if she is getting more upset by the minute. A few moments later I hear a small mechanical sound coming from our front door. Looking at the door, **I SEE IT!!**

First, I see the top deadbolt's keyhole turn itself and unwind as it pulls the lock out of the latch from the front door. Then I watch as the second keyhole, does the same. I sit in disbelief and stunned silence. My mouth open wide and gaping. The third keyhole opens itself, and finally, the bottom shiny brass doorknob twists with a small squeak, as it unlatches and the front door blows open. Gypsy raises herself up from her lowered position nearer the tile floor, and ferociously starts barking at thin air.

No one is there!

LEAVING 2095

After all my relatives leave my graduation party, I know this will be my last day and night in the house. Good old 2095 in Troy. *Will I miss this house?* Maybe someday I'll miss it; but for now, I can't wait to get on with my life and get away from the haunting. I'm anxious to walk away. I wonder what it will be like living in a house that isn't haunted.

My mother made it clear that if I were to stay, I would have to pay her rent and go to the nearby community college, which I didn't feel was right for me. I already applied and have been accepted into University of Cincinnati, so I am moving out. Can I afford it? No, but I'm going to make it work!

I picked out an apartment, with the help of my boyfriend and his mother, for fall when school starts, but tomorrow I am off to Washington, D.C., to spend the summer living with my older sister. I transferred my job at the *Holiday Inn* in Tipp City, where I had been working for a few months to Chase, Maryland, to work at the BIG HOTEL. The plan was to save money all summer.

****

As all my guests continue to file out our front door, I bid them good-bye and smile. *Who knows the next time*

I'll see them again, or even IF I'll ever see them again.

After they've all gone, I clean up the dishes and put away the food by myself. I don't call out for Mom. I'm assuming she's worn out from the day's events and already in bed.

I finish cleaning and walk down the dark hallway once more to my bedroom and pack up the rest of my stuff. I know if I leave it at the house, I will probably never see it again. Mom has a tendency to "Goodwill" everything.

As I pack up, I think of all the years I have spent in this house. The past year had been tragic. I lost my dog, the pet I had since I was 6 years old. I also lost my grandfather, who I really loved and looked up to. On his death bed, he turned to me and told me how proud he was of me and how he loved my boyfriend, Kevin, and how he knew Kevin would take care of me. My grandfather said he would always be there, watching over me and guiding me.

I thought of the day we moved in and how scared and angry I was at my father for separating from us and making us begin this new life that I didn't want.

I thought about poor Mrs. Walter and about seeing her that day as I was sitting in front of the television, and Zander cried and screamed in terror. She looked so kind as she made us peanut butter and jelly sandwiches. I thought about what Heather had said and how she had tried to scare my friend, Stacey, and me that afternoon. I thought about Emily and me and our awful hallway experiences.

I remember my mother's keys and the mimicking sounds that started each night precisely at 9. *I believe it's Mrs. Walter just wanting some attention.* Then I thought of the weird experience I had when I saw my mother and interacted with her, and she acted as if she didn't know who I was. Then I chased her into her own bedroom to find her in a nightgown and sleeping. So it couldn't have been her at all! I still didn't understand that night and wouldn't even know what the word "doppelganger" was until I was out of college and had children of my own.

Then my thoughts drifted to Lexi and how she had ruined my 16ᵗʰ birthday party. I remembered her séance and the evil she brought into my house. I still wish I would have ended our friendship long before that incident. I always felt so stupid for keeping her as friend when she was such a horrible person. I always felt guilty for some reason. *I still can't believe she ruined my birthday.* Some SWEET SIXTEEN! What can I say, some girls get cars, I got an evil entity brought into my house to knock me out. *Yay… NOT!*

Suddenly, I remembered the misty-white baby doll figure that appeared when I woke up in the middle of the night. I still don't know what hit me on the head that night and probably never will. But I will never ever forget it! It was the most CHILLING thing I have ever seen! *And I've seen a lot in THIS HOUSE.*

Zipping up my suitcase, taping up all my boxes, and marking them with the items inside, I make a pile of all my things in the foyer. I stop and look at the front door. Zander left for an overnight visit with our dad, who came for my graduation.

I WILL MISS HIM MOST OF ALL…!

I look at the front door remembering all the times my boyfriend came through it. I remember how Mom had scared the heck out of poor Kevin last Christmas when she hung a singing wreath on our front door. When Kevin knocked, the wreath burst into a Merry

Christmas song and we all laughed. It was hysterical!

There sure were good times, but also bad ones. Bad–like when the door would unlock on its own and our collie would bark, then she would run down the street; Mom would have to fetch her to bring her back home again. *It sure was an interesting house.*

"Becca?" my mother calls to me from her bedroom. "I'll be out soon, then we'll order a pizza for your last night."

"Okay, Mom!" I say in surprise. I thought after this long day she would be out. *Awe… my last night. Wow…*

"Did you do the trash? It's coming tomorrow."

Wow, there's something I won't miss. Taking out the trash! I think to myself, as I walk into the kitchen and call back to her, "No, but I am now!"

As I pull the bag from the large white trashcan, I think of all the years that have gone by and why I must have lived through it … to learn something, I suppose. Right? Isn't that why people live through bad things? It must be a test from God. *Maybe I've gained some serious wisdom from this house and these strange experiences,* I think to myself as I close the trash bag with a twisty tie and head for the garage door.

Reaching the garage door, I open it with my empty hand. I am not prepared for what I see. I stand there stunned, too shocked to scream, not wanting to see what I am seeing. I try to close my gaping mouth, only to have it immediately fall back open.

There, hanging by a handmade black thin noose, is the women I saw in our kitchen years ago, smiling and making us sandwiches. She was dressed in jeans and a sweater. Her blue eyes bulging out of her head as if she were staring straight ahead, looking at our garage door. Her garage door.

An image that will forever be burned into my brain.

Without warning, a small draft comes through the cold, gray closed garage and her body turns to face me. Her eyes blank, her short brown hair tattered and pulled up from the back by the noose that choked her. You could see her small feet, with her brown leather shoes dangling under her swaying body. She is lifeless and pale, as if she's been dead for hours, but I just discovered her. Here, in the place she loved. Her house. 2095.

"Becca," my mother's voice invades my trance. She must have come into the kitchen and wondered why I was still standing in the doorway of the garage, trash bag in hand. "I figured you had taken out the trash by now. Is everything alright?"

"Yes," I reply. "Yes, it is, Mom. Everything is just fine," I assured my mother and I stepped into the garage to find that Mrs. Walters was gone.

AFTER LEAVING 2095

I had just turned 19 and moved out of the house, 2095, in Troy that May 1999, the day after I graduated from high school and moved to Washington, D.C., to live with my sister for the summer. In the fall, I came home briefly to see my mother and ended up staying with my boyfriend's parents down the street because my mother was moving out. She was going to sell the house and I didn't want to be in her way. A week later, I was in my new apartment in Cincinnati where I lived for 2 years while attending college.

My mother remarried in 2000 after she sold the house.

I later moved to Maryland, where Kevin got a job while I finished college at the University of Maryland. Then we moved back home to Troy.

One Halloween, I was sitting with Kevin and some friends at a local restaurant when my friends started telling ghost stories about places around town. For the first time in my life, I was unable to stop myself. I blurted out, "Ghost stories? Ha! You want to hear a REAL ghost story? I can tell you about the haunted house I grew up in. I saw some serious stuff in there!"

I don't know what I was thinking. All my friends turned and looked at me completely stunned. But then a total stranger, who was sitting next to my friend at the bar waiting for the bartender, turned to me, and said, "You wouldn't be talking about the house at 2095 would you?" I was flabbergasted. I had been waiting for this day to come since I moved back to Troy. Being in a small town, news travels fast, so I knew it was only a matter of time before I heard from someone. But a total stranger? Wow!

"Yes." I said completely serious as I looked at him. All my friends followed our conversation intently as it unfolded.

"My wife and I looked at that house with our real estate agent last week. We had a crazy experience!" His expression was completely serious as he continued.

"We walked inside and were in the front foyer near the door and there was a big brown Rottweiler lying in the middle of the tiled floor. It wouldn't move! We actually had to step over it because it didn't budge. We only knew it was awake because its eyes were open. So, we just stepped over it and thought, '*Okayy…*'"

The stranger kept going, "I just had an eerie feeling. Anyway, we started to walk around the house. But while we were walking through the family room and into the kitchen, we felt like something was following us. It was as if someone was constantly watching. I really can't explain it; it was just strange. Then something unexplainable happened."

"As we came out of the dining room, circling back into the foyer, we saw that the dog that had been lying on the floor was now standing up and had its head real low. It was growling and staring at us. It hadn't moved before and didn't seem fazed when we stepped over it. But now it was up and growling. It was really weird!"

"We all looked at each other and were afraid to move." He continued, "We asked the agent if this was normal and if she had been in this house before.

She said not in a few years, but she hadn't met these owners. 'They didn't even tell me they had a dog. Normally, they disclose that so we're aware of a dog in the house. Most people put their pets in a cage, or in the garage during a showing.' Then she started to take a step forward and that's when it happened," he said.

"The dog's head suddenly began to rise up as it made a strange noise. Then, its eyes zeroed in on us, as it began throwing up everywhere and its head turned in a 360 DEGREE FULL CIRCLE!! Vomit was flying everywhere, all through the air at us."

"Oh my, God!" we all said in unison.

"Yeah, we screamed and ran out of the house. The realtor was freaking out in the car. Her professionalism went out the window after that and we ended up switching realtors. It was just too weird to see her again," he replied.

"I have to ask you, did you ever have anything weird like that happen when you were living there?" asked the man, finally flagging down the barmaid and getting his tall ale refilled.

"Yes," I said. Then I told him about my dog Gypsy barking at the door after seeing it unlock itself and fly open once a week. I told him about how strange it was that she would bark at thin air as if she could see someone there, but we clearly couldn't. I also told him that our dog would then take off down the street and my mother would have to fetch her.

"Wow," said everyone, including the man holding his beer. "That's nothing!" I assured them. Then the man bid us good-bye and went to tell his wife about meeting me. I never saw him again, but I remember his story to this day.

Epilogue

21 YEARS LATER

Four years ago, after writing the prologue to this book, I sat in front of my old house, 2095, angry, emotional, worried, and full of regret and Catholic guilt. I started writing this book as a form of therapy; but along the way I learned it was so much more than that!

I first interviewed all of the neighbors who knew Julia Walter and her family and knew what she had been through. I asked them all, "Do you know why she killed herself?" The answer to this question was my mission. I had to find out *why*.

As a mother, I didn't understand how you could fathom taking your own life when you had three children. *How could you be willing to miss being a part of your children's lives as they grew up? How could you miss all the important things in their lives? Their graduations, weddings, their children being born?*

All our neighbors described her as a very nice, caring, and loving person, who was overwhelmed by her children who didn't treat her well. The children were rather mouthy and abusive toward her. They all said that it was her son, in this booked renamed, Kyle, who drove her over the edge after they moved.

The other consistent fact – Julia loved that house. She had it blessed and invited the whole church and some neighbors. She loved the town. Troy had become her home. And the transfer, along with her son's behavior and the other children's abusive treatment, pushed her over the edge. Mentally, she just couldn't handle it anymore. But what was the real story?

While researching the property and finally finding Julia's obituary, which was oddly hard to track down, I finally did find out the facts. Julia didn't kill herself in my house, but in her new house, 23 days after selling the home she loved and moving! I also requested her death certificate to confirm. And yes, it all was correct.

So Heather, my babysitter in this book, did tell me and Stacey some misinformation, but that was probably because she was a teenager who didn't know all the facts, and she probably was trying to scare us a little. She was, after all, a teenager.

A year ago, I went to a convention in Cincinnati. I was still writing my book and had it with me because I heard a publisher was coming. I wanted to be able to show it to her. Unfortunately, she didn't make it due to a health emergency. So, there I was walking around this convention by myself. The friend who had come with me and was ahead talking to someone, when a woman I had never seen before, emerged from the crowd came over to me and said she had a message for me. She sat me down and told me that Julia Walter was happy that I was writing her journey and I was going to save lives with my book and prevent others from making the same mistake. She said that we were put together for this reason. She also said that since I left 2095, that Julia had always guided me.

I almost died myself! I immediately began to cry. First tears of relief, then tears of sadness for Julia. And then I did the most important thing. I let go of my guilt for not being able to help her while living at 2095 all those years ago. I always begged my mother to get a priest in from our church. Julia had also been a parishioner there, so I thought the priest could help her get out of the house. I feared she was stuck! I always felt guilty for not being able to have the power to help her! But in that moment, all my pain and guilt disappeared. *I never thought that would happen!*

I thanked the woman, then tried to tell her my story, but she said she already knew it because Julia told her everything. *Julia already told her. WOW!* The woman also said she knew I felt Julia when writing this book (*which is also true!*), and that by writing this book she has been freed from the house, after all those years. This brought me to more tears.

While writing this book, I felt as if I could feel Julia's wants and needs as well as woes. The woman I met assured me that was the case. She told me my feelings and instincts were correct.

I was telling my story, Julia's story, as she wanted it and felt it. My research, interviews, and discussions with her husband's co-workers and my past neighbors supported every emotional path Julia led me on.

I have tried my best to be accurate in telling her story to save lives. Which I hope this book does. So please heed Julia's lessons. If you have depression or family troubles and need help, there is *no* shame in getting it. We don't know if Julia regretted her choice to end her own life, but her friends and family regret not knowing how bad her depression was.

In 1987, we didn't have mental health support

services like we do today. Julia really didn't have an outlet.

Another reason I wanted to write this book is I wanted to express to others who may be of the Catholic faith, like myself, that it doesn't matter what religion you are. Sometimes God just works in mysterious ways. So, don't ever say all ghosts are evil, because now I know that isn't true. Sometimes they just need something or someone to tell their story. I truly believe that God was the one who brought us together for this very reason. So I could write Julia's story and possibly save lives.

Also, my mother did the best she could given the circumstances. She was probably overwhelmed and did not know what to do. I don't blame her and now understand it was God's will.

Thank you everyone for joining Julia and me on our journey. Embrace whatever lesson you may have gotten from our experiences.

-Rosella C. Rowe

About The Author

Rosella C. Rowe is a paranormal investigator in Ohio and who loves to write paranormal thrillers. She has written The Haunting at 2095 and has a well known blog, My Haunted Travel Blog, and is the host of A Haunting Good Time Radio Show.

Rosella has years of ghost hunting and investigation experience in the paranormal field traveling around the U.S to the most haunted-historic locations and writing about them in her blog. Rosella prides herself on telling the real story and truth regarding her ghostly experiences with spirits she encountered at historic locations, as well as the legends that surround the entity.

When Rosella was a child she encountered a woman who killed herself 23 days after moving from the property Rosella lived in. This experience spiked a chilling interest in the paranormal world. Since then, Rosella has been researching, traveling, and writing about the paranormal.

Rosella's new paranormal thriller coming soon is: *911 Emergency* about a female police officer who happens on a bad car accident in the woods of her hometown. When she stops her car she hears a spirit call out to her for help only to find a tall dark shadow person who follows her home, haunts her, falls in the love with her, and tries to break up her and her new boyfriend. Rosella is also working on a third book called: *Paranormal at the Victorian House Museum*.

Rosella has made many TV and Radio appearances around the country and has been featured at the world's largest book festivals in: Savannah, Miami, New York City, Italy, China, and Germany.

For More Information:

Author Website:
www.RosellaCRowe.com

My Haunted Travel Blog:
https://myhauntedtravelblog.blogspot.com/

A Haunting Good Time Radio Show:
https://anchor.fm/rosella-c-rowe

Social Media Pages:
Facebook: @RosellaCRoweAuthor
Twitter: @RosellaCRowe1

CPSIA information can be obtained
at www.ICGtesting.com
Printed in the USA
BVHW040801270522
638090BV00006B/322